Big Bad Love

Also by Larry Brown

Facing the Music

Dirty Work

Stories by Larry Brown

Algonquin Books of Chapel Hill

1990

Published by
Algonquin Books of Chapel Hill
Post Office Box 2225
Chapel Hill, North Carolina 27515-2225
a division of
Workman Publishing Company, Inc.
708 Broadway
New York, New York 10003

Two of the stories in this book have
appeared previously in slightly
different form: "Sleep" in *The Carolina
Quarterly* and "Big Bad Love" in
The Chattahoochee Review.

Design by Molly Renda.
Jacket art by Glennray Tutor.

Library of Congress Cataloging-in-Publication Data
Brown, Larry
   Big bad love : stories / by Larry Brown. — 1st ed.
        p.   cm.
      ISBN 0-945575-46-7
      I. Title.
   PS3552.R6927B5   1990
   813'.54—dc20   90-34411CIP

10 9 8 7 6 5 4 3 2 1

First Edition

Contents

Big Bad Love

Falling out of Love

Sheena Baby, the one that I loved, and I were walking around. It was late one evening. All the clouds had gathered up into big marshmallows and mushrooms, and it was an evening as fine as you could ask for except that we had two flat tires on our car some miles back down the road and didn't know where we were or who to ask. Besides this main emergency, I knew things weren't right. We were about ready to kill one another, and I've spoken on this subject once before.

Sheena Baby was LOVE, a sex-kitten goddess. I'd loved her for a long time, ever since I'd gotten rid of Miss Sheila, and I felt like I'd given part of myself away. Sheena Baby didn't hurt for me like I did for her. I knew it. I'd thought about shooting her first and me second, but that wouldn't have done either one of us any good. It wouldn't be nothing but a short article

3

in some paper that strangers could read and shake their heads over, then turn to the sports. Love goes wrong. It happens every day. You don't need to kill yourself for love if you can help it but sometimes it's hard not to.

If we'd had inflated tires I could've got her off over in the woods somewhere, put some Thin Lizzy on, told her how we could work it out. Told her not only to be my baby but to be my *only* baby. Later, in the dark, we could have moved together. But she didn't love me, and I could see that finally, so I decided to be real nasty to her.

I said: "You just don't want to listen to anybody."

She said: "I've bout had it with your goddamn mouth."

"Jam it," I said.

"Kiss my ass," she said.

"Make it bare," I said, hoping she would, but she didn't, and we walked off in different directions.

I didn't know why something that started off feeling so good had to wind up feeling so bad. Love was a big word and it covered a lot of territory. You could spend your whole life chasing after it and wind up with nothing, be an old bitter guy with long nose and ear hair and no teeth, hanging out in bars looking for somebody your age, but the chances of success went down then. After a while you got too many strikes against you.

I didn't know what to do, where to go. We were miles and miles from any town, anybody who might have flat-fixer services and could perhaps send a tow truck. I could see myself walking for days, sleeping in the ditches. I knew the first man who came along would pick her up, but I doubted that the first woman who came along would pick me up. I turned around and looked at her. Sheena Baby was getting smaller in the distance with each step, and I could see that fine ass she had wobbling. I knew she'd wobble it harder when she heard something coming down the road. She wouldn't even have to stick out her thumb since she already had plenty of other stuff sticking out, and I couldn't see myself doing without her for the rest of my life. I'd finally found the one I wanted, and now she didn't want me. I knew I'd done it to myself, staying up all hours of the night playing *Assorted Golden Hits* and cooking french fries at two a.m., and letting the garbage pile up in the broom closet, not keeping my toenails cut short enough and scratching her legs with them at night in my sleep. It looked like when you first met somebody everything was just hunky-dory, and then you got to know each other. You found out that in spite of all her apparent beauty she had a little nasty-looking wart on her ass or she'd had six toes when she was born and they'd just clipped it off and then you got to wondering about genetics and progeny. You woke up in the morning before she did and leaned over and smelled her breath and said, *Jesus Christ what the hell did you eat?* Stuff like that broke the illusion, and formed opinions were changed when you really got to know somebody, when you lived with her and saw her in the morning and noticed that the backs of her thighs had little ripples of fat on them.

I wanted to run after her, though, because I loved her the way she was and I knew that nobody was perfect, especially not me, but I also knew that when a person found out how bad somebody else wanted them it automatically turned them

5

off and they would begin to put distance between you, since
the hunger one person has for another is seldom shared
equally between them. It was sad, and it was messed up, but
I had to figure a way out, because she was walking back the
way we'd come, all the way back to Oxford, looked like, if she
had to, and I needed two tubeless tires mounted and inflated
pretty fast, or at least patched, and I needed a jack, and a
four-way lug wrench, none of which I had. We'd gone out
without those amenities, just for a short run to the beer store,
and then picked up some Budweiser and things deteriorated
from there. Went riding. Said fuck it. Decided to wait until
later that evening to cut the grass. The *smallest* laid plans of
mice and men.

An argument arose, one that had been brewing, about me
talking to some chick a few nights past in a bar, somebody
who'd seen some of my work. I'd warned her about that,
about how I couldn't avoid that, and for a while she'd seemed
to understand. She even suffered their phone calls for a while,
various ladies calling at all hours of the day and night.

But then she got to saying, "*Another* call for you," handing
me the phone with a tight-lipped smile, pulling up a stool to
watch me while I hunkered down over the phone and spoke a
soft and inquisitive hello into the mouthpiece, and listening
to every word. She wanted the number changed. I didn't.
She wanted it unlisted. I protested. People needed to get
ahold of me for consultations, estimates, I told her. They need
to get ahold of you for other stuff, too, looks like, she said. It
got pretty bitter. We started fighting. We'd have to make up
before we could make love, and that's always a killer. It got to

killing the sensitivity between us, and once you get that eating at you, you're a prime candidate to end up chasing somebody down a road, like I wound up doing that evening.

She kept walking and I started walking after her. I was trying to get close enough to call out to her. I knew it would sound awful, and you know it would if you think about it, but I knew too that she'd probably just ignore it, keep on walking, do me like that.

It kind of reminded me of being at the Memphis Zoological Gardens one time, years before, before puberty hit me. I was walking around with a balloon on a stick in one hand, a cone of cotton candy in the other. I was just wandering, and wandered over near the bear pits, where a large group of people had gathered. They were large bears, I don't know, brown, or maybe grizzly. Something was going on, you could tell. The bears were down in a large pit with rocks and an artificial pool and an artificial cave, living out their artificial lives. People were pointing down into the pit and grinning. I pushed my way up through the crowd to see what was happening. Fathers had children sitting on their necks, holding them by their legs. There were two bears down in the pit, big fuzzy things. One of them was standing and the other one was lying on its back with its front paws up in the air, waving its head around and looking at the people. It looked a little drunk.

I looked at the bears and looked at the people and then looked at the bears again. The bear that was standing put its nose between the hind legs of the bear that was lying on its back and took a long hard sniff. The bear that was lying on its back raised its head and curled its lips out in a long tunnel and said *ROOOOOOOOOOOOO!* real loud. The bear that was standing raised its head and shifted its feet and stuck its nose between the other bear's legs again and the bear on its back waved its forepaws when the other bear took a long hard sniff and said *OOOOROOOOOOO! MOOROOOOOOO! GROOOOOOOO!*

The people grinned and pointed and the bear that was standing wiggled its nose and stuck it back between the other bear's legs and took another long hard sniff and the bear on its back closed its eyes and waved its head and said *BROOO-OOOOOOOOOOOOOOOOOOOO!* Then the bear that was lying on its back got up and licked the other bear for a little bit, they both did, then they slowly turned together and went into their cave and out of sight. The crowd kept looking. I did, too. The bears didn't come back out, though. I felt, even way back then, that something strange and mysterious was going on, something we weren't going to be allowed to see. The crowd drifted away after a while, in ones and twos, then threes and fours, until I was the only one left. I kept watching the dark mouth of that cave, but there was nothing to see except the black air inside it, and shadowy forms slowly moving in there. After a while I went away, too, and left them alone.

I suddenly remembered all that, going down the road after Sheena Baby, the way you will. I was afraid for some stranger to pick up Sheena Baby, because I didn't know what he might do or try to do to her. These days, you don't want to be hitching rides with strangers. There's too much that can happen. I didn't want to see anything worse than me befall her. I was bad enough, and I knew it, and I wanted to be better to her, try and rectify things if only I could. But she seemed to be walking faster, and I wasn't getting any closer to her. My legs were hurting, and it was hot, but there was some beer in the car. She'd already passed it but I was getting closer to it. I finally reached it and stopped to take a breather beside it, and saw the cooler in the floorboard and said, Well, hell, as long as I'm here.

We'd conveniently had our two flats under a shade tree, and it wasn't bad under those large reaching limbs. It was almost cool, and the beer was cold, so I helped myself to one and sat down on the side of the road, leaning up against the car. It gave me ample time for reflection. You can figure out just about anything if you get ample time for reflection. You can sit back then and get the big picture. I opened that beer and took a long cold drink of it, then lit a cigarette, and the world didn't seem nearly as bad then. There were some other trees on the side of the road, and it was nice and shady, and there was a little ditch with some frogs sitting in it. It was kind of tranquil. I thought, Well, what if she does leave me? Is it the end of the world? No, it wasn't the end of the world. The world wasn't going to roll off its axis just because somebody had a broken heart. The sun wasn't going to stop rising. I asked myself if it would be painful. Yes, it would be painful. It would hurt for an undetermined number of days or weeks. If I was lucky it wouldn't hurt for the rest of my life, but there was no telling how long it would be until I found another one as good as her. They didn't make them like her every day. I looked up the road. She was gone.

I sat there and drank beer for a while, smoked cigarettes.

It wasn't a bad way to while away the time. I didn't know what to do about the car (it was her car). I didn't want to just leave it. I didn't know but what there might be vandals about, unlawful guys who might strip off the wheels and rip off the radio/tape player, make off with the battery. I didn't want to sit around there and watch it all night, though. So I got to looking at the car. Both the flats were on the driver's side. And suddenly the idea came to me, Why don't you just drive it like it is, but *real slow*? It was such a good idea I couldn't figure out why I hadn't thought of it before. I had read somewhere that you could drive on a flat for ten miles if you drove real slow. I knew that even with two flats I could probably drive it faster than Sheena Baby could walk, and that I might eventually catch up with her. So I got in the car and put the beer between my legs. I turned the key and it cranked right up. It was just sitting a little low on my side. I knew it looked a little ridiculous, probably, and I hoped nobody would drive up behind me and start hooting at me.

I turned around slowly in the road, testing the feel of it. It felt a little bumpy. The thought came to me that I might be ruining the tires, but I just got another beer out when that thought hit me.

I tried to see how fast I was going once I got straightened out and headed after Sheena Baby, but I was still in low gear and the speedometer was just bumping up and down between 0 and 5 mph. I figured Sheena Baby was probably walking about 2 or 3 mph. I wondered: Could I shift into second? I did. The tires went to slapping a little faster. The needle rose to nearly 10 mph. I smiled. I knew I'd overtake her before long.

I turned on the radio and tried to find a little music. I put my sunglasses on. I felt like I was making some real progress.

The last time I'd been in Sheena Baby's car there'd been two or three joints in an empty Marlboro pack in the glove box. I flipped it open and the Marlboro pack was still there. I elbowed the wheel and peeked inside the pack and, sure enough, there were still two whole joints in there. I got one out and put the other one back up. Things were getting pretty groovy. It was a Sunday evening and Army Archard was counting down all the top 100 hits of 1967. I lit that joint and bumped down the road drinking my beer and keeping time on the steering wheel, holding the smoke in deep. After a while I was just shaking my head over how good it all was. I listened to Jimi Hendrix and Janis Joplin and Elvis Presley and The Doors and Cream and Grand Funk Railroad and CCR and Percy Sledge, wawa wawa wa. I got to singing out loud and moving my shoulders around and when that joint got short I took little tokes and got all I could out of it. Army was breaking in once in a while, commenting on how fine it all was and talking about how lucky we'd all been to be alive in that era. I agreed with him 100 percent. I wished I'd gone out to San Francisco and worn flowers in my hair. I wished I'd been hip instead of picking cotton. All of a sudden it didn't bother me any more that Sheena Baby was leaving me, and I saw that it had been inevitable. We were two different people. We came from different backgrounds, and our interests were not similar. It was a wonder that we'd stayed together as long as we had. Love took a lot of different forms and sometimes what appeared to be love wasn't really love at all, was just infatuation in disguise. It hurt when that happened, and it messed you up for a while, but sooner or later you got back on your feet and faced the world and saw that love was hard to find and sometimes it took some looking. Love wasn't going to just walk up and slap you in the face. It wasn't going to tackle you around the knees out on the sidewalk. Love wasn't going to leap out of a second story window on top of you.

I rode along there, slightly bumping, the needle wobbling between 7 and 10 mph. The tires went whop whop whop, and the rubber squirmed under the iron rims, and it made the car rock gently. I knew I was going to make it. I knew all this was just a temporary setback.

Army Archard kept playing those great hits from 1967. I kept drinking that beer. There was plenty more in the cooler. I had plenty of cigarettes. I saw a figure walking along the road, growing larger as I got closer, and I beat time with my hand on the steering wheel and slapped the floormat with my tennis shoe. I knew she'd feel funny when I bumped by in her car. It hit me too that I'd go home and sleep alone, that I wouldn't have her arms around me to hold me in the night, not have her arms any more forever.

Her arms, any more, forever.

I slammed on the brakes right beside her. She stopped walking and turned and looked at me. We looked at each other for about a minute. There were a lot of things I could have told her, a lot of promises I could have made and broken later, just anything to get her back in the car. But all I said was, "You want a ride?"

She didn't say anything when she got in. She shut the door

and knelt on the seat across from me, with her fine thick legs folded up under her, deeply tanned, muscled as hell, a body-builder with fourteen trophies. I was skinny, coughed in the mornings, had a lot of gas most days. Her eyes were close to me, staring into mine, deep blue and beautiful. She came to me. She came to me and she wrapped her arms around me and squeezed me (she could bench two hundred) tight. She mashed her lips down over mine and crushed my mouth tight against hers and pushed me back against the door and I could hear her breathing hard through her nose. She was sucking all the air she could and kissing me as hard as she could. My side of the car was low and she was on top of me, trying to climb up into my lap, pawing at me and hugging me alternately, pushing me hard against the door. The door opened and I fell backwards out into the road and Sheena Baby crawled down from the car on top of me except for my feet, which were still in the car, and she laid down on top of me, kissing me, pushing the back of my head down hard on the asphalt, mashing my ears between her two hands, panting, forgiving all, covering me completely with love, blocking out the sun with it, there beside a flat tire and the rusty under-side of the car on the open road where anybody driving by wanting a testament to love could ride by and see it, naked, exposed for the whole world to view.

That was when the cops pulled up, two of them, with hard faces and shiny sunglasses, and I saw with a sick feeling in my heart that our happy ending was about to take a turn for the worse.

The Apprentice

This can't be living. I drink too much Old Milwaukee and wake up in the morning and it tastes like old bread crusts in my mouth. All my underwear's dirty, I can't find my insurance policy.

Here I was thinking we had a good normal marriage. She dirtied up my car and changed the TV channels for me, and I'd bring her Butter Pecan Crunch home from Kroger's. I'd tell her to just leave the dishes until tomorrow, things like that. I didn't even say anything when her dog pissed in my chair. For better and for worse and all that. I even nursed her in sickness once.

Judy wanted to be a writer. Writewritewritewritewrite. That's all she studied. She was always writing something, and always wanting me to read it. Hell, I'd read it. Some of it. I'd tell her it was pretty good if it was. Only most of the time it wasn't. I'd try to be honest. She wrote this story one time about a man whose wife was always speeding and getting tickets. This woman would get three or four tickets a week. She'd come home and tell her husband about the tickets, and he'd raise hell with her. This went on for a while. The tickets were piling up. They owed something like sixteen hundred dollars to City Hall. So finally the guy decided he'd do something about it. He killed his wife. Blew her head off with a shotgun, and then confessed to the whole thing. When the cops found him he was wiping up her blood with the old traffic tickets. Terrific story, right? I told her I didn't think much of it, and she got pissed off. That was the thing of it. If I told her I liked one of her stories, she'd pin me down on the couch with the story in her hand and try to get me to point out every paragraph, every sentence, hell, every *word* I liked. And if I didn't like it, she'd sulk around the house for three or four days. There just wasn't any pleasing her.

She didn't want to have children yet. There was plenty of time, she said. Wait till I sell my novel, she said. I even took this high-paying job, working inside a nuclear reactor, so she could quit the post office and write full-time. I didn't mind. I didn't even mind having to eat TV dinners by myself sometimes. I mean, if you love somebody, you put up with them. Hell, I told her to go for it, grab all the gusto she could. But even that wasn't enough. When we first got married, we'd go to a movie every Friday night. Then on Saturday night, we'd go out somewhere with some of our friends and listen to a band, have a few drinks, do some dancing and just kick up our heels.

And then she started writing. She wrote a novel first. Blasted straight through, seven months, night and day. I'd be in there on the couch watching old Hopalong Cassidy or somebody and hear that typewriter going like an M-60 machine gun in the bedroom. That's where she writes. I'd stay in there by myself until the movie or Johnny Carson or whatever I was watching went off, and then I'd get up and open the door and ask her if she was ready to go to bed. And most of the time, she'd say she was right in the middle of a scene and had to finish it. She'd give me this sort of pained but patient expression that said clear as glass, Shut the door and leave me alone.

What the hell. We had some fights about it. Anybody would. We had some knock-down-drag-outs. I busted a picture that her mother gave us over the goldfish bowl one night, and another time I kicked a hole in the bedroom door after she locked me out.

And that wasn't the worst of it. All our friends started wanting to know why we never went out with them any more. The only thing I could tell them was that she was working on her writing. I hated doing that. You tell people something like that and they look at you like you're crazy. I mean, who sits around writing fiction besides Edgar Rice Burroughs or Stephen King, or in other words, somebody who knows what the hell he's doing? I used to tell her that shit. Especially if she'd just written something I didn't particularly like. Like this one time, she wrote a short story about a woman who was a hunchback. She called it "The Hunchwoman of Cincinnati." *It wasn't worth a shit!* I didn't want to hurt her feelings, but it was boring as hell. And the whole time I was reading it, she was sitting right beside me on the couch, sipping a glass of wine, smoking one cigarette after another. She was looking over my shoulder, trying to see where I was on the page. This damn woman who was a hunchback had a son who was a cripple. The only thing he was good for, apparently, was shoveling out horse stalls. But every night he'd bring his little twopence or whatever home. I think it was supposed to be set back in olden times or something. They were trying to save up enough money for an operation. But she didn't say *who* was going to get the operation, the woman or the kid. That was the big suspense of the whole crappy story. It turned out they had this damn *dog* you didn't even know about until the last page, and the dog had some rare disease that only this veterinarian in Cincinnati could cure, for—you guessed it—the exact same amount this kid made after working for a year shoveling all this horseshit. I damn near puked when I got through reading it.

But I didn't say anything when I finished it, not right away. I got up and went into the kitchen and got a beer. I still had on my radioactive work clothes. She hadn't even given me time to eat my supper. I was trying to think of some nice way to bring her down, but hell, I didn't know what to say. She was sitting on the couch with her legs tucked underneath her, grinning. Sipping that wine, smiling like the cat that ate your sardines.

"Well?" she said. "What did you think of it?"

She leaned forward a little on the couch and held her wineglass between her hands. I told her I didn't know. I told her I thought I ought to read it again to sift out the ambiguities and decide which mode of symbolism the denouement pertained to. I took some English Lit classes in college and that was the only thing that saved my ass that night. It was like old times when we went to bed. She came twice. She said I was the greatest husband and the most understanding human on earth. I felt like a real bastard.

The next morning was Saturday, and I didn't have to go to work. I remember waking up and thinking about a little early morning love, but then I heard the typewriter pecking. I dozed off for a while because I didn't want to be by myself all day. Saturdays she wrote all day. When I got up and went into the kitchen to make coffee, it was already made. There was bacon laid out on a paper towel just as pretty as you please, hash browns and scrambled eggs on the warmer on the stove, and my plate was set with the morning paper folded right beside my cup. She had butter and biscuits and molasses on the table, just like in a restaurant. I really felt like a bastard then.

I didn't know what to do. If I said it was bad, she'd sull up or maybe cry. She cried a lot when I didn't like her stuff. And if I said it was good when it really wasn't, she'd get very encouraged and sit right down and type it up all nice and neat and send it off to *Playboy* or somewhere, and then get all broke down when it came back rejected. I used to hate mailtime on Saturdays, when I was home. About eleven o'clock, if she had a story out, she'd sit down on the couch and open the drapes on the front window, watching for the mailman. She'd sit there with a cup of coffee in her hands. She'd start doing that about three days after she'd sent a story off, I think. I guess she did it every day while it was out. I don't know. But I'm sure she did. She wouldn't even write while she was waiting for the mailman. When she was waiting for the mailman, she wouldn't do anything but look out the window. Every once in a while, she'd get up and go to the front door and open it, and look up the street to see if she could see him coming. And finally, there he'd be. She'd get up and get over to one side of the curtains, and peek out to see what he was pulling out of his bag. If it was just some small stuff, some white envelopes, or circulars from TG&Y or somewhere, she'd rush out as soon as he put the stuff in the box. But if she saw him pull a long brown manila envelope out of his bag, she'd jerk the curtains back together and sit down fast on the couch and put her face in her hands.

She'd say: "It came *back*," like she was talking about a positive test for cancer of the womb. She'd sit right there and shake her head and never lift her face from her hands.

"I don't want to go out and get it," she'd say. "Lonnie, you go out and get it."

So I'd go out and get it. What the hell, it was no big emotional experience to me. Just a piece of mail. That didn't mean I didn't know what it meant to her. I knew it hurt her to have her stuff come back. But *Playboy* is never going to publish something like "The Hunchwoman of Cincinnati." Never. Ever. Not in a million years. I'd bring it in, and she'd be sitting there. She wouldn't look at me. She would have turned on the TV by then. She'd be looking at it like she was really interested in it. We had this routine we'd go through. It was always the same thing.

"You want to open it?" I'd say.

She'd shake her head quickly, violently almost.

"*No!* You open it."

I'd always tear the damned thing opening it, and she'd scream, "Be *careful!* There might be a *note* in it!" She meant like a note from an editor.

Of course there never was. There was never a note from *Playboy* inside the envelope. Big Daddy Hugh had never taken the time to tell her he was dying to see something else she'd written.

"Open it slow," she'd say. "Look in."

I'd open it slow. I'd look in.

"Do you see anything?" she'd say.

I always said the same thing: "Yeah, I see something."

"What?"

"I don't know."

"Is it a note?"

"I don't know."

Then there'd be this small period of silence. She'd lean forward and turn down the volume on the TV. She'd look over at me like we were about to be gassed and only had a few remaining moments between us.

"Look," she'd say.

I'd reach in and pull it out. "The material enclosed has been given careful consideration and is not suitable for use in our publication at this time. Due to the volume of submissions received, we regret that we cannot offer individual criticisms. All submissions should be accompanied by a stamped, self-addressed envelope if their return is desired.

Your interest in blah blah blah is most warmly appreciated. The editors."

And then she'd go off on a crying jag. She'd just get up and rush off into the bedroom and throw herself on the bed. So I didn't want another one of those scenes coming up that Saturday morning. She didn't have anything out right then; she'd sent some stuff off to *Redbook*, but they'd rejected all of it. I think she'd already gotten about fourteen rejection slips when she wrote "The Hunchwoman of Cincinnati." I was sitting there eating my breakfast when she came in. I had the story beside my plate. I'd been reading it over again, but it didn't look any better than it had the night before. As far as I could tell, the kid was a nerd, and his mother was a turd, and the only thing the dog did, even on the last page, was lie around and whine and thump "its tail weekly against the hard unforgiving gray cobblestone pavement littered with cruel gray pigeon droppings."

"Well," she said. She was grinning again. "You've slept on it."

Yes I had.

"I didn't know you knew so much about literature," she said.

"Ah, I'm a closet fan of Flaubert's."

"Who's he?"

"Gustave. I like Melville, too. You ever read *Moby Dick*?"

"No, but I saw it on the late movie. Gregory Peck and all them. Did that come from a book?"

"Yes, it did, dear. A very great book."

"Well, I didn't know it was a book. What'd you think about my story?"

I knew that if I said I liked it, she'd ball my brains out. She'd shut down the typewriter, lock all the doors and pull the curtains closed, strip naked down in the floor and tell me to climb on.

"It was something else," I said. "Indescribable."

She started stripping out of her clothes.

"Unbelievable."

She stepped out of her panties.

"I can't believe you wrote it."

She got back on the pillows of the couch and put one foot on the coffee table and said, "Come and get it, big boy."

"You're better than Jackie Collins," I said, and went to her.

Okay, so it was a lousy thing to do. But it made her happy, for a while at least. Naturally she typed up a clean copy of "The Hunchwoman of Cincinnati," didn't change a word, and sent it off. I think it set some kind of record for coming back. I came home from the reactor one evening and she was drunk in the living room. She had a bottle of vodka, a pint, and she was halfway through it. She had it mixed up in some grape Kool-Aid, and she was soused. Supper wasn't fixed, and she started getting sick, and I wound up holding her head over the commode for her while she threw up.

All this happened before things got bad.

I really got into that first novel she wrote. It was about this grizzly bear in Yellowstone National Park that had lost its fear of humans and was running around eating everybody. The story line was pretty good, even if her dialogue did suck, and

she somehow knew how to make all these narrative hooks.
For instance, getting one of the characters into a tight squeeze,
then cutting to another chapter so that you'd rush along to
see what was going to happen. And she invented all these
people. That was what amazed me. She just made up all these
people out of her mind. I mean people that were nothing like
us. It was all about these park rangers who were trying to kill
this bear. Most of them had bad marriages, but one of them,
this young guy named John, was a newlywed. He was a real
upright guy, loved his wife and all that, was dedicated to the
Park Service. But his buddy, Jesse, had this wife who looked
like Ann-Margret and was always coming on to him. Okay.
Then, there was this other ranger named Walker, who'd
already been dipping his wick into Jesse's wife, Glenda, and
this Walker dude was sort of nuts. But he kept it carefully
hidden. He was a big muscled-up mean motherfucker with a
temper like a short fuse. John had this other friend, Ben,
who knew what was going on between Walker and Glenda,
but he didn't say anything. (You know how that shit goes if
one of your friends' wives has ever been messing around on
him and you didn't want to tell him. I mean, you're sort of
caught in the middle. You can tell your friend, and risk him
knocking the shit out of you and calling you a liar, or keep
your mouth shut and feel like a bastard for not telling him.)
So that's what old Ben was going through. He had a wife, too,
but she was almost nonexistent in Judy's novel. All these park
rangers were running around trying to kill this man-eating
bear, and the bear was killing their dogs and eating campers.
They had a bunch of close encounters with the bear, missed

some shots and things, and then close to the end of it, old Jesse went one-on-one with this bad Ursus Horribilus, missed his shot, and got killed. Very painfully. That was a heartbreaker. I liked old Jesse. And right after that, old Ben amost went crazy because he hadn't told Jesse that Glenda was messing around on him with Walker. And then he really went crazy. He beat the shit out of this *other* dude named Tommy, who'd been messing around with Glenda a few years before, and they kicked him off the Park Service. And see, that left John and this maniac Walker to kill the bear. I didn't know what was going to happen. I imagined all sorts of bad things happening. What I figured was going to happen was that Walker was going to rape John's wife, and John would come in and catch them in bed at the same time he found the bear going through the garbage in his back yard, and there'd be this big incredible scene of bloodshed and retribution right at the end. But the ending was so disappointing that I don't even want to talk about it.

She built me up for a big letdown. It pissed me off. But I didn't know what to say to her. I mean she came so damn *close* on her first try, and then screwed it up at the end. The ending just left me hanging. But naturally she flew into a big flurry of typing and typed it all up, didn't change a word, and sent it off to Random House. Excellent choice. One of the biggest publishing houses in the world. And guess what? It came back with a *note*. Somebody had scribbled in at the bottom of the rejection slip, *suggest you send this to a paperback house*. She freaked out. She ran around *showing* that damn note to people and calling everybody. And then she sent it off to seven other places and they all rejected it. I think it cost us about forty-seven dollars in stamps. And then she gave up on it.

"Give up on it?" I said. "What the hell for? After you spent all that time on it?"

"It's not any good," she said.

"Well, it's not the worst thing I've ever read. I think you just need to fix up the ending a little, maybe cut it some, work on the dialogue."

She just sat there with her arms crossed and her legs crossed and looked at me. I could tell what she was thinking. There I was, the non-writer, trying to tell the writer how to write.

"I used to think it was good. Now I don't."

"*Why?*"

"It's hard to explain," she said. "The more I write, and the more I read, the more I see how bad I am."

"Well hell. What's the use of keeping on, then?"

"Because. The more I write, the better I'll get."

"When?"

"In a few years."

"Years? How many years?" I wasn't sure how much more radiation my system could stand.

"I don't know. Nobody does. But I'll know it when I get there. Now run along, hon. I'm working on a new story."

"What?" I said, and I couldn't help it. "'Cinderella and the Four Flashers'?"

I didn't look at her face before I slammed the door.

. . .

I didn't mean to be mean to her, hell. But my sex life was practically nil. Oh, sometimes we'd have a quickie, just before she went to sleep, but most of the time she was just too tired. She worked like a dog, and I started working more overtime just so I wouldn't have to sit around the house by myself. When I got home I'd smoke a joint and watch TV. I'd watch Buck Rogers, anything. I couldn't play the stereo because she said it bothered her.

Sometimes she wouldn't even eat. She'd get up in the morning and have a piece of cheese toast or something, and she'd go until supper without anything else. She started losing weight, and I bitched at her about that. That made her mad, and she'd retreat into her work. One thing caused another, and sometimes the only time we spoke to each other was during arguments.

But she was getting better. There was no denying it. Sometimes in the morning when I was getting ready for work and she was sleeping, I'd read part of what she had written the night before. You could just see the things the characters were doing, and why they did them. But she got to where she didn't like for me to read her stuff, said it wasn't good enough yet, and she'd hide it.

It wasn't just the sex. I mean, I loved going to bed with her, but more than that, I loved *her*. I wanted to *hold* her. Just kiss her. I wanted to spend time with her and talk to her, and I wanted us to be just like other married people we knew. But we weren't like them. We stayed in separate rooms and only slept together. Half the time I'd have to go to bed before her, because I had to get up. She didn't have to get up. All she had to do was write and sleep. And I guess I began to get a little bitter.

I started going out at night. She didn't seem to care. She'd be sitting at her typewriter when I left, and most of the time she'd still be sitting there when I came back in. Or if she wasn't, she'd be in the bed asleep. I was hardly ever seeing her. I never saw anybody so obsessed. Her appearance went to shit, and she'd dress in the first thing that came to hand. Sometimes she wouldn't even get dressed, just sit there and work in her nightgown.

And then she started getting published. One story here, another one there. The first acceptance was a great event, and we were happy for a few weeks, and she wanted to throw a big party and invite all our friends. But some of them didn't show up, I guess because so many of them felt that they had been left by the wayside. I understood it. I told Judy that you couldn't keep friends like a can of worms and just open the can whenever you needed them. I said that to her after everybody had left, while we were standing in the kitchen after cleaning up the mess. She smiled a strange little smile, and went behind the closed door, and her clattering machine.

Nowadays I don't expect too much. She doesn't ask me to read her stuff any more. I get up and go to work, have a few beers with the boys afterwards. I come in and go in there and peck her on the cheek, then find my supper in the microwave and punch the button to start it. I might have a beer or two after supper, or read a little.

I love her is the thing. I've tried to stop loving her, I've even tried seeing other women, but it never did feel right, so I quit it.

Sometimes she'll surprise me. She'll have a big candlelit dinner fixed, or step into the shower with me when I'm least expecting it. I don't know where this writing thing came from or what caused it, but it's a part of her now, like her arms or her face. Success for her isn't a matter of if any more. It's just a matter of when.

Once in a while, just for fun, I pull out "The Hunchwoman of Cincinnati" and read it. It's got to be the worse damn thing I've ever read. But I'm sort of beginning to like the dog.

Wild Thing

She came into a bar I was in one night and she took a stool. I noticed the tight jeans, the long brown hair, the pretty red blouse. A woman like her, you have to notice. That's what you're sitting in there for.

I noticed that she looked around to see who was in the bar. There weren't many people in there. It was early yet. So I began to wonder about her. A good-looking woman, alone in the early evening in a sort of redneck bar. I guess she felt me watching her. She turned to look at me, and she smiled for several seconds, and then she leaned over and spoke to the bartender, who soon brought her a beer.

I'd been out of things for a while. I was having trouble with my wife. One of the things that was wrong was that I was spending too many nights away from home, and it was causing fights that were hard for me to win. It's hard to win when you don't have right on your side. It's hard to win when you know that your own fucking up is causing the problem.

Boys from work, some friends I was supposed to meet, they hadn't shown up. I had a table to myself because it was more comfortable than a stool. A basketball game was on, with the sound off, lots of guys jumping around, other people like me watching it. I looked at the bar and tried to see the woman's face in the mirror behind the bottles. She didn't look old. Sometimes at first glance the bodies look young, but the faces, on closer examination, are not. This one didn't look old.

I sat there without watching what was going on on the television screen. I didn't know why I didn't just get up and go home. I could see them all in the living room, sitting in front of the television without me. My wife would be in the bed asleep when I went in, probably, if she wasn't sitting up waiting on me. There were times when I couldn't stand to stay there. Leaving the house like I did made it hard on everybody. I knew the kids asked her where I went and why I went. I didn't know what she told them. I didn't want to think about what she told them. I knew if I kept it up they would stop asking after a while. I knew that would be as bad as anything.

She kept sitting there, looking around a little, smoking a cigarette. After a while she got down off her bar stool and went to the jukebox and dug some change out of her pocket. Her jeans were so tight she had trouble getting the money out, like she'd been melted and poured into them. I watched her. She leaned over the panel of bright lights and set her beer down and held the cigarette between the fingers of her left hand, moving her head a little to what was already playing. And she turned around and looked straight at me and asked me what I liked. I smiled, told her to play E19.

"What's that?" she said, through the music. I picked up my beer and went over to her. That was the start of it.

She smiled when she looked down and saw that it was Rod Stewart and Jeff Beck on "People Get Ready." I stood beside her and pulled some quarters from my own pocket. I could smell the light fragrance of her, and I pointed to some other good ones. She took the quarters I handed her and told me how sweet I was. Her face was happy and animated, and I could feel us making a connection already. All I had to do was be halfway cool, maybe not tell any stupid jokes, ask her about herself, and let her tell me about herself, since self is everybody's favorite subject and they'll think you're a brilliant conversationalist if you get them started talking on that. We played Journey and Guns N' Roses and Randy Travis and Joan Baez and Sam Cooke. Then I told her to come on and sit down with me.

More people came in but I didn't notice them. I kept ahead of her drinking-wise so that I could keep paying, and after three I looked around and saw that the bar was full of people. I didn't tell her that I was married and she didn't ask. She kept talking to me, leaning over toward me, pushing one strand of her long brown hair back to the side. She worked in a factory somewhere in town at a desk and a computer and she had moved here recently, she said. We got closer and closer and she put her hand on my arm. We laughed and drank and listened to the music.

Later I asked her if she wanted to go for a ride and she said yes. I had some beer iced down in the trunk. They got a crazy law in this county. You can't go in a store and buy cold beer; you can only buy it hot. So you have to get a cooler and keep it in the car. You have to always be thinking ahead. We left together, her holding onto my arm, her leg brushing mine, people I knew watching.

She sat close to me in the car, her hands touching me. We left town and went out into the country and rolled the windows down. She dug in her purse and held up a twisted length of grass in a pink paper and I nodded and smiled. After that the music never sounded better. We rode nearly to the end of the county and I stopped on a bridge and got us another beer out of the trunk and she sat in the car while I stood near the rear fender taking a leak. The night was clear, all the stars out, summer on its way. I got back in the car and she was all over me, hands, mouth, I don't know how long it went on right in the middle of the bridge. Finally I pulled away and told her that we had to go someplace else. She asked me if I knew of such a place. I said yes I did.

It wasn't too far from there, up a winding old road with gravel, an old house place with just the chimney sticking up among the stars when we pulled up. I pushed the lights off. Everything was slow and clear because of the grass. When I killed the motor I could hear everything. Bullfrogs sounding in a pond down in the woods. Whippoorwills calling in the trees. The sound of cars somewhere, far off. She came to me and I held her and she put my hands on the places they wanted to be. When I kissed her she went back on the seat and pulled me down on top of her. She was more than eager. She seemed desperate. And I was the same way.

She was tight, so much that it hurt both of us for a while. I even asked her if she was a virgin but she said no. She was smooth and fine and her skin was silky and warm under my hands. Then a car drove up. I saw the lights in the tops of the trees, raised up and saw two headlights coming slowly around a curve. We had to try and find our underwear in the floorboard and our pants and the car kept coming while we jerked things on and then it stopped and just sat there with its lights shining on us. I had one sock on and no shirt. I don't know what she had on.

"I thought you said this place was safe," she said.

"I thought it was. Hell. I don't know who this is."

The car sat there. I went ahead and put on my shirt and pants.

"Shit," I said. I cranked the car and turned it around and pulled up beside whoever it was. The car kept sitting there. I couldn't see anybody inside. It was like nobody was driving it. Then we went on past it and out of sight.

She didn't say anything for a while. I stopped a mile or two down the road and got us another beer from the trunk. I handed her one and she took it silently. Owls were hooting out there in the dark beside the road. She opened the beer, lit a cigarette, and just sat drinking and blowing smoke out the window.

Finally she said: "Next time we'll get us a room."

Right, I thought. Next time. Nah. There wouldn't be a next time.

The lights were off at the house. She'd even cut the carport light off. Easing in, or trying to, I bumped into things. There wasn't even a lamp on. And then suddenly there was, with her hand on it, and the quick furious anger all over her face.

"Where you been?" she said.

"Riding around," I muttered.

"You know what time it is?"

I was heading into the bedroom with my shirt already unbuttoned, but I stopped and looked back at her.

"No. What time is it?"

She tapped her foot on the floor and reached for her cigarettes.

"You can't keep on doing me like this," she said.

I was tired and I didn't want to hear it. All I wanted to do was close my eyes and try to sleep a little before the alarm went off.

"Okay," I said. "Okay. Now please let me go to sleep."

I left her in there, smoking, tapping her foot. I went into the dark bedroom, where my baby son was sprawled in sleep in the middle of our bed, and I took my clothes off, lay down beside him, touched his hair and the side of his face. I loved him. I knew what I was doing to him. He never moved. I thought of how horrible my life was and then I closed my eyes. Just before I drifted off to sleep I was vaguely aware of her getting into bed. She didn't speak, and the next thing I knew the alarm was going off.

. . .

I decided not to go to work that day. I have the kind of job where I don't have to be there every day, and people working for me who can take care of things. I wanted to go fishing. I wanted to be on a boat in a lake with a pole in my hand and crickets or minnows in a bucket or a box and a cooler full of cold beer to help me think over everything I needed to think over.

Later that day I was on the lake, in the boat, a beer in my hand, fishing. I eased up to a stump where I thought a few crappie might be hiding out. I caught a little minnow from the bucket, put the hook through his back, and lowered him down to meet some of his big brothers. It kept going down, never did stop, and I pulled in one that weighed about two pounds. I had another cooler with ice just for fish and I put him in there. It looked like I was going to lay them in the shade. But after another hour, I hadn't caught another fish. I fished up, down, all around, changed minnows, squirted on Mister Fishter, did everything I knew, and still I had just that one fish in my cooler. Finally I let my cork rest and took stock of things.

I was fucking up with these other women. I wasn't spending any time with my kids. My wife and I never spoke to each other hardly unless we were arguing. I couldn't stand to stay home, and I hated myself every time I went out. Now I'd met another one, and she seemed wonderful except for the car pulling up and catching us, which hadn't been her fault. I wasn't catching any fish, and since it was only ten o'clock in the morning, I knew that if I kept drinking beer I was headed for a bad drunk sometime later that day. Possibly even a DUI conviction. For the moment I was safe. I wasn't driving anything but my boat, and they couldn't get me out there, unless it was some gung ho officer of the Mississippi game wardens, and I knew all of them. I knew I'd probably be facing another bad scene when I got home, whenever I got home. I knew I could probably make everything right by going home with a big load of fish and dressing them and cooking a good supper for my whole family, but the problem was I'd only caught one and it didn't look like I was going to catch any more now that I'd started drinking beer. There comes a time some days when you say fuck it, and I didn't know whether to say that that early in the morning or not. I hated to. I'd said it so much in the past and it hadn't ever helped anything. It looked like the whole problem was with me, looked like my wife could just keep rocking on the way she was until she was old and gray and sixty and I couldn't. It seemed like we were raising our children simply for their own benefit and not for ours. But our own lovemaking had brought that. Now it seemed we'd locked into a position that was far beyond our imaginings when we'd married, and there didn't seem to be any recourse. Be born, live, bear children in turn, get old, die. There didn't seem like there ever was anything else. And there didn't seem like there ever was anything else since man had been man, since the first primitive ape-person—was that Adam?— crawled down from the tree and found a female under another tree and hauled her away to a cave, where he ravished her. I was uneasy about a lot of things, my own mortality among them. I didn't know if when I died I was going to die forever, or maybe just for twenty years, and come back as a house cat or something. The whole universe was a secret to me, including what happened over there in Siberia in the 1920s when something hit the ground and knocked all that timber down and set all those woods on fire. I was uneasy about the Bermuda Triangle, and how long I could keep getting up and getting it up, and afraid I'd never find the best woman in the whole world for me to love. I decided I'd better just keep drinking beer and keep my hook in the water and hope for the best.

It was nearly dark when I got home. I had three miserable fish, and all the ice I'd had on them had melted. Still, I was determined to cook fish for my family. My wife was just walking into the carport with a basketful of clothes. The kids were playing ball in the yard. Me, I was pretty drunk.

My wife came up to me and tried to kiss me and we messed around some right there in the carport and she got hot, and before I knew it we were back in the bedroom with our clothes partway off, bumping together like two minks. That was when one of my kids shot his head around the side of the window where we'd been in too big a hurry to close the blinds and said, "Hey, Dad! Want to pitch a few balls?"

He slunk away, with many looks back. I got my clothes on and got the hell away from there.

Some more nights later I was in the bar again and I saw her come in again but I didn't look at her and she did her jukebox routine again without my quarters, but with glances over her shoulder at me several times. I was nursing a beer.

I'd been sitting there thinking about things for a while. I wasn't too keen on going back to work the next morning, and was pretty sure the boys could handle it for a few days without me. I knew she was going to sidle over, and pretty soon she did.

"What you got the blues about?"

"Nothing. Sit down."

"We gonna do it again tonight?"

"I don't know if we will or not."

"I wish we would. It was good the other night till them people drove up."

"I don't know if I want to or not."

"I wish we would."

"I don't know."

"Please."

"Since you put it like that."

We wound up back in the same place. I knew that lightning didn't strike twice, that I couldn't be unlucky two nights in a row. We shucked down, were moving and grooving and saying baby baby baby when the lights came around the curve. I sat up in the seat and reached under it for my pistol, told her I was getting a little tired of this shit. I had just my pants on when I stepped out of the car. I had that little hogleg down beside my leg. Somebody threw a spotlight in my face and told me to freeze, and I heard a couple of shotgun safeties snick off real soft.

"Just hold it, boy. Now turn around. Now drop that gun. Now spread out on the fender there."

I got frisked while she was putting her clothes on and she

was fully dressed by the time they decided to shine their lights on her. They weren't pissed that I had the gun, they were just pissed that I'd messed up their dope surveillance, and when they went to looking through her purse I had a few bad moments, but it turned out that she'd wisely hidden her joints inside her panties, and being the Southern gentlemen they were, they weren't about to ask her to disrobe again. They told me they'd appreciate the shit out of it if I'd find someplace else to park because they were working on busting some people right there and they were sure I didn't want to be mixed up in it. I told them Nosir, Budweiser was my only vice. We booked on out of there, and I think it was like 3:47 when I got on in home, after we'd finished with a motel room we'd used for twenty-four minutes.

I got on my forklift the next day and drove it all around the plant. We had to load a bunch of dishwashers and it took all day. I thought I never would get out of there. But finally the day ended and I just had enough time to get to the Little League game, where all the upstanding other fathers were standing around watching their kids swat, and there I sat, mired down in a lawn chair, digging out quarters for Cokes and popcorn, getting depressed when my own small slugger struck out or missed making a catch. It was a hard life, and I didn't know if I was going to be able to keep on living it.

My wife came over and sat down next to me and said: "What you doing?"

"Nothing."

"You want to take the kids out to eat after the game?"

"Not really."

"What you got planned?"

"Nothing."

"You don't enjoy this, do you?"

"Not really."

She looked at me. "You hate being married, don't you?"

"Why do you say that?"

She looked back at the game. "Because. I can tell."

I watched them play for a while. Mothers were yelling. Once in a while a pop fly would sail over the fence. One kid got hit in the eye and started crying and had to be replaced. They gave him a towel with some ice in it, and somebody else held his hand and bought him a snow cone.

"You want a divorce?" she said.

"Not really."

"Well," she said. "I hate you're so unhappy."

Then she got up and left me sitting there.

We happened again about a week later. I'd had two beers and she came in. She didn't even mess around with the jukebox, she just made a beeline for me and got me by the arm.

"Come on over to my house," she said.

I thought, Hell's bells. Thought, Why didn't we do this before?

We rushed on over there, to a darkened apartment, and stumbled in, pulling our clothes off and kissing in the living room. She couldn't wait for the bed, had to get down on the couch. She was moaning, and stuffing a pillow into her mouth, and that's where we were when a vehicle pulled in up front, shining lights in through the picture window, all the way through the curtains. She started making some frantic motions but I thought it was just the heat of passion. Then the lights went off. They don't have adequate parking in those places sometimes anyway, but the car door slammed so hard I thought something about it, and the next thing I knew the front door was opening and the light was on in the living room and there we were, with a big maniac with a lug wrench coming toward the couch. I jumped up and threw a pillow in his face, and he knocked the stuffing out of the couch where my leg had been. She screamed while he was calling me 900 motherfuckers, and I saw he was fixing to kill me. My dick was waving around in front of me just briefly. I didn't mess around with any diplomacy, I picked up a kitchen chair and hit him in the face with it, and the way the blood flew was awful. I called her about 900 different kinds of bitch before I got my clothes on and got out of there, but I did get out of there, hoping like hell he wasn't dead.

I didn't know what to do after that, whether to go fishing or just say no to everything. I wanted to run off. I even figured out how long I could live in another town with the money in my checking account. But he didn't know me, and I didn't know him. Of course he'd seen my face, some of it anyway. He'd be trying his best to hurt me real bad for sure if he could. Somebody busted my face with a kitchen chair, I'd be looking to return the favor.

So I stayed home. Didn't go out and hit any bars. I hung around the house and watched TV, drank coffee on the couch.

Helped the kids with their homework. Played Daddy. I came in before her a couple of times and started supper and put clothes in to wash. Mopped the kitchen floor. Dusted the furniture. She got to glowing, and things were great between us in bed. But I wanted that other one again because it was different and it was dangerous now, and so the peace and tranquility only lasted about a week, nine days tops.

The last time I saw him, he came in the bar with her. I was sitting at my table in the corner, back to the wall, watching who came in the door. They saw me about the same time I saw them. She was drunk on her ass. They went to the bar but he eyeballed me, wouldn't turn his back on me. Smart move. I saw him checking the exits. He kind of straddled a stool. They ordered drinks and the drinks came and she paid. I was wondering what to hit the son of a bitch with this time. There wasn't anything in there but cue sticks and balls. There was probably a shotgun behind the counter, but I knew I'd never make it to that. There was always the side door, but I didn't think I was quite ready for that. I wanted to see what her act was, what the game she was playing was, what I was gambling with over a small piece of nearly skinny ass.

I got up and put some money in the jukebox and sat back down. *People get ready* . . . And then Jeff Beck cut loose and filled the whole place up with his guitar. The people shooting pool moved to it. The drunks sitting around the bar wished it was them playing it. She swayed on the barstool and looked over her shoulder at me and winked, and his beer slammed down, and he was coming, and I picked up the wooden chair I was sitting in and gave it to him, this time straight across the teeth.

Nobody said a word when I walked out with her, especially not him.

We found some place off in the woods again, not the same place, not her house, not a motel room, just a place off in the woods. Crickets were chirping. Coon dogs or fox dogs somewhere were running. She fed the end of the joint to me and I fed it back to her and, while all that was going on in the face of what all had gone on, I wondered: what was the purpose? But I didn't want to think about things much right then. She laid those lips on me, and we moved down in the seat, and I knew that it wouldn't be but a little bit before those headlights, somebody's, would ease around the curve.

Big Bad Love

My *dog* died. I went out there in the yard and looked at him
and there he was, dead as a hammer. Boy, I hated it. I knew
I'd have to look around and see about a shovel. But it didn't
look like he'd been dead long and there wasn't any hurry, and
I was wanting a drink somewhat, so I went on out a little
further into the yard to see if my truck would crank and it
would, so I left. Thought I'd bury the dog later. Before Mildred got home. Figured I had plenty of time.

Birds were singing, flowers were blooming. It was just wonderful. I hated for my old dog to be dead and miss all that,
but I didn't know if dogs cared about stuff like that or not. I
didn't have a whole lot of gas in my truck. I didn't figure I
needed to get started riding and drinking. I thought I'd just
ride over and get something to drink and then ride back, sit

on the porch and maybe cut my toenails until Mildred nearly got home, then start burying the dog to occupy myself.

Joe Barlow wasn't home. I sat in front of his house for three minutes and blew the horn, but nobody came out. I left there and went to U. T. Oslin's house. The whole place was boarded up, looked like nobody had lived there for three or four years. Weeds were all up in the yard and stuff. I left there and went by Manley Musgrove's, but I figured he was asleep and didn't want to wake up, so I just spurted on past his house, didn't stop.

I'd had that old dog for a long time, from way past my first marriage. I was sure going to miss him. He had a few little idiosyncratic oddities about him that didn't exactly endear him to some people, like rolling in fresh cattle droppings and then climbing up on somebody's truck seats if they left the door open. Mildred had always been after me to shoot him, but I never had. He was bad about pointing baby possums and then catching them and dragging them up into the yard and then eating them, and Mildred was always so tender-hearted she never could stand to see a thing like that. She just never had seen her cat in action, though, the one she'd let in the house to pet and sleep on the couch, get hairs all over the throw pillows. That thing had a litter of kittens last summer, and I was standing out there in the yard one day while she had them stashed under the corn crib for safekeeping. I'd been out in the vegetable garden cussing and mashing cutworms off my tomatoes. I'd cuss those little fellows and pick them off and mash each one under the heel of my tennis shoe. Those little things were green and they had green guts. That cat went out in the garden for a minute and come back carrying a little baby rabbit in her mouth. It wasn't dead. It was still kicking. What she was doing was training her babies to be killers. She laid that baby rabbit down right in the middle of those baby cats, and they didn't know what to do with it. Of course the baby rabbit was squealing right pitiful and all and it ran off first thing. The old mama cat ran out there in the yard after it and caught it again. Brought it back. Set it back down in the middle of those kittens. They started trying to bite it and stuff, growling these little bitty baby growls. That baby rabbit jumped up and ran off again. I stood there and watched that and thought about cats in general, and about what that baby rabbit was going through. She caught it and brought it back again and laid it down in the middle of her litter. They had enough sense to bite it some then, and it squealed some more and then jumped up and took off running out across the yard. Only it couldn't run too good by then. She ran out there and caught it again, brought it back. They went to gnawing on it again. It jumped up and ran off again. She brought it back again. It was getting slower each time. I thought, Yeah, I ought to just go in the house here and get me about four rounds of Number 6 shot and load up my Light Twelve and clean these sadistic creatures out from under my corn crib. The only thing was they kept the rats away and I guess a man has to give up one or two things to get another thing or two, but I went and got me a hammer handle and put that baby rabbit out of its misery. I used to raise them a long time ago, rabbits. I was pretty familiar with the rabbit family. They were so cute when they were little. Just little balls of fur. They'd hop around there in the cage, eating lettuce, plus I fed them Purina Rabbit Chow, and they grew pretty fast on that, and it wouldn't be but about eight weeks before they'd be ready to kill. They'll dress out about two pounds of meat at that age. By then your doe's bred again and expecting some more or maybe even having them by then, and they'll eat you out of house and home if you don't harden your heart and take eight or ten of them and a hammer handle out behind the corn crib and knock them in the head. I had some neighbor kids then. They played with those rabbits all the time. They'd hold them up beside their cheeks and just smile and smile and rub that fur with their faces. And here I was out behind the corn crib while the kids were in school, knocking rabbits in the head and dressing them and then telling the kids they got out of the cage and ran away. It finally made me so uneasy and torn in different directions I had to quit it. I gave my doe away and turned the buck loose, I guess the coyotes ate him. I was thinking about all that while I was riding around, looking for a drink. I knew Mildred wouldn't be happy to see that dead dog in the yard. I knew she'd be happy to see it dead, only not in the yard.

I ran up on a Negro fishing by a bridge and stopped and hollered at him and asked him did he have anything to drink. It turned out it was Barthy, or Bartholemew, Pettigrew, a Negro I'd been knowing for most of my life. I had even picked some cotton with him a long time before, in my teenaged years. He didn't want to let on like he had anything to drink, but I knew he did because he always did. He was an old-timey Negro, one that wouldn't give you any sass. Of course I don't think one man ought to have to bow down to another one because of the color of his skin. But I had to get down in the creek with him and squat down talking to him before he'd even let on that he might have *anything* to drink. And what he had wasn't much. Three Old Milwaukees in some cool water that his minnows were swimming around in. We talked about cotton and cows for ten minutes and corn some, then finally I gave him a dollar and got one of his beers. He didn't know where U. T. Oslin was.

By the time I'd gone about a mile I'd finished half of that one. I knew that wasn't going to get it. I had a dog to bury, and I knew it would take more than one half-hot Old Milwaukee. I checked my billfold and I think I had four dollars. I kept driving slower and drinking slower, but the closer I got to the bottom, the hotter it got. I drank the rest of it and chunked the can out the window. I would have loved to've had about a cold six-pack iced down, and about ten dollars worth of gas in my truck. I could have rode and rode and drank then. I decided I might better get back to the house and see if I could find my checkbook.

Mildred wasn't in yet. My old dog hadn't moved any. I poked him a little with my tennis shoe toe. He just sort of moved inside his skin and came back to rest. I estimated the time before Mildred would be home. I judged it to be about forty-five minutes. That was enough time for a shower, piss on burying the dog. I figured I could do it when I come back in. I'd already taken that first drink and I wanted another one. And I told myself it wasn't every day a man's dog up and died.

I run inside and showered and shaved and slapped some shit on my hair. I drove uptown and wrote a twenty-dollar check at Kroger's, picked up a hot sixer and a one twenty-nine bag of ice. I knew Mildred would be perturbed when she saw that I was out loose again. Lord love her, she had trouble keeping me home; her puss was just not that good. And so I would have to strike out occasionally, for parts and places unknown.

There was a nice place on the other side of town that didn't look cross-eyed at country people coming in there just because they didn't have a whole lot of class. The only thing wrong with it was that sometimes the people who came in there had so little class that often they would get to arguing and begin to shoot and cut one another. They wouldn't do it when they were sober, it would just be after they were drinking. I figured it would be a good place to be sitting on a stool right about that time, before they all got to drinking heavy.

I parked my truck under a tree and went inside that establishment and it was dark and cool, like under a corn crib would be. I knew I had that six-pack to drive me all the way home. Mildred was sexually frustrated because of her over-large organ and it just wore me out trying to apply enough friction to that thing for her to achieve internal orgasm. So, it was titillating for me to sit on a stool and talk to the young waitresses who served drinks and just generally fantasize about their young normal organs and wonder what they would be like, although it was guilty work and unsettling and morally not right.

I ordered a beer, spoke to everybody in general, lit a cigarette. I felt quite at home. I had on a clean shirt and my teeth had been brushed. I saw by my wristwatch that Mildred would be pulling into our driveway in about five more minutes. My beer arrived and I held it up high in the air and, saluting, said, "Here's to Mildred." Several people looked at me funny.

This particular bar had a lot of red velvet in it. It also had numerous mirrors that looked like they had been splattered with gold paint. It was quite classy, particularly for a place that had so many people with so little or no class come into it.

After I drank a little, I went over to the jukebox and put some money in to help pass the time and help take my mind off thoughts of Mildred. They had fourteen Tom T. Hall songs, and I played every one of them. It seemed to put everybody in a good mood. I noticed several people looking at me kindly, as if to say thanks for playing all that Tom T. I knew that, by then, Mildred had seen my dead dog. I didn't want to think about it, and I didn't know what she would think about it. I knew that she would be unhappy with me for not going ahead and burying the dog, and also for being out late drinking and riding. We had been over this thing many times before, and we weren't getting any closer to a solution. I just couldn't do anything with her big Tunnel of Love. I could hit one side at a time, but not both sides. I didn't feel like this was my fault, since I, like many other men or nearly all men, played high school basketball and football and baseball and hockey and have taken many showers with naked boys and know by casual observance that I am adequately hung. Perhaps even well hung. I have seen boys whose peters looked like acorns. Mildred would not have even known one of those boys had it inserted. I would have had to be the Moby Dick of love to adequately satisfy Mildred. But I had sworn before God and Church to always cherish her and I supposed I would always have to. I did not cherish my first, other wife; I threw her over for Mildred. But it did not keep me from wanting something a little different from the feeling of sticking my equipment out the window and having relations with the whole world.

I got back on my stool and drank a little more and thought about the time Mildred and I discussed corrective surgery for her deformity. Mildred, I should point out, had the most wonderful ass. That was the original point of interest that attracted me to her. I have seen men pant, looking at her in a bathing suit. Mildred was always naturally hot-sexed. I knew it had to be frustrating for her to be like that. But she said she would be absolutely mortified to have to undergo an operation of that nature or even discuss it with a doctor or nurse. So, sitting there on that stool, I didn't know much other way to turn. I knew she wasn't going to like that dead dog lying in our front yard. I thought, Hey, baby, what about your cruel cats?

By the time I'd had my second beer, I'd thought about going home and hauling the shotgun out and killing every cat on the place. The last time I had counted them, there were lots of them. Rats and mice were no longer a problem. I was sure those rodents came up on the edge of the yard, took one look at all those cats, and said: No way, José.

Often people in bars don't speak to one another, and often this is what happens to me. I am extremely friendly. I just don't know what to say to people. I didn't know what to say to Mildred the first time I met her. I met her in Destin, Florida, and saw that wonderful ass she had. She did all the talking. I was down there recuperating from my divorce that was almost pending. I was separated from my first wife, but divorce was not pending. It was just almost pending, and I was trying to recuperate from that and was going home to try and patch things up in a few days. When I saw Mildred, everything went out the window, good intentions, everything, the divorce became pending. Mildred represented herself as a virtuous woman with naturally hot tendencies and told me sincerely that she was technically a virgin, but on our wedding night I quickly formed the erroneous opinion that this was simply not the case. As a matter of fact, I thought on our wedding night that Mildred's puss had simply been worn out from numerous encounters over a period of many years with some enormous number of men, which caused me and Mildred to almost divorce the next day, until she broke down crying at the Continental breakfast and confessed that I was only the first and one-half person to ever penetrate her. I took that as a compliment to mean the other person had only made it in halfway.

By the time I started drinking my third beer I had thought a lot about Mildred's womb and had begun to wonder if by some lucky chance she ever got pregnant would the baby fall out prematurely. I wondered if any of the other men in that bar were facing that particular problem and didn't figure they were. What I figured was it was a unique problem but not quite out of line with the rest of my life. It seemed for some reason or another I had always been given the short end of the stick. I knew that it had nothing to do with my nature or character and was just an unlucky streak of fate, just like when I had fallen off the persimmon tree limb four feet off the ground at my grandmother's house and broken my arm and missed my own birthday party, then got back later with the cast on and there were only crumbs of cake in puddles of ice cream that flies were walking over on the picnic table, with all my little friends gone and all the toys and presents un- wrapped and already played with.

By the time I started drinking my fourth beer I did not give much of a damn whether I ever got any more of Mil- dred's puss or not. I knew that she had been home for quite a good while by then and was probably wondering where I was. I knew that she had probably already fixed supper and had noted my dead dog in the yard and was probably sitting out on the front porch looking for me to come in. I began talking to some young women shooting pool and took up a stick myself and shot about three racks of eight ball with them, losing all three for a dollar. I was merely hustling these young ladies and trying to get a line of trash going. I thought I could lure some of them off with the promise of a cold sixer in my truck later.

By the time I started drinking my fifth beer there were several long-haired tattooed muscled young men who had come into the place and they had scabs on their arms and boots and overalls on. They didn't appear jocular and they looked like they had been out in the sun all day, working very hard. My skin was milk white and I had seven dollars left in my pocket. I knew it was about time for me to get in the road.

I went outside and got in my truck and got out of town quickly. I hated to think about my old dog lying there in the yard, unburied. I thought I might ride around for a while and think about him, and Mildred, but I didn't know what good it would do. I had considered sending off for one of these pump-up penis deals but I thought they might be dangerous or at the least would not work.

Within ten minutes I was away from town and out on a back road that didn't have lawmen patrolling it and I felt free there to open another suds I had iced down earlier. I knew that Mildred would want me in the bed beside her as soon as I got home, and I wasn't looking forward eagerly to that. I felt like all our ministrations to each other were headed to a dead end and that nobody would care fifty years in the future what we had gone through. It left me feeling a little bit depressed and fearful, and I kept drinking, faster.

I rode for quite a while. I saw some cows loose from a pasture and weaved in among them. The locusts had crawled out of the ground after thirteen long years and when I stopped to pee on a bridge I thought my truck was still running because of them. They were beyond any loudness of bugs I had ever heard.

I had put away about eight beers by that time. My blood alcohol content was probably in the .10 range or maybe a little lower or higher. It didn't actually matter. Squeezing her legs together didn't help matters any at all. It was hopeless. I

didn't know what to do and I didn't want to go back home. I
kept riding, drinking, riding. I thought maybe I might run
into somebody. I knew I'd eventually have to bury my dog. I
knew she was sitting out on the porch, waiting on me. Watching all the lights coming down the road, wondering if each
one was me. I felt sad about it and bad about it. I opened
another beer and realized the folly of not stopping by the
liquor store while I was in town and purchasing a half pint of
peach schnapps to go along with my nice cold beers. I delib-
erated for several minutes over this dilemma and found it was
probably an oversight on my part. I did not want to go home,
neither did I want to be indicted by the Mississippi Highway
Safety Patrol for Driving Under the Influence of alcohol. I
observed that I was driving fairly straight and I had not slurred
any words yet to my knowledge. Quite the opposite, in fact,
and my eyes were not red and my blood pressure did not feel
elevated. I felt that a short run back to town would not have
astronomical odds in favor of my being overtaken after a high-
speed pursuit. I turned around at a small place on the road
and began to retrace my route back to civilization.

I returned to and from town without incident and once
more resumed my erratic wanderings over country roads near
my home. The evening hour had begun to wane and it was
nearly dark. I knew if I stayed out much longer there would
be some dramatic scene with Mildred upon my arrival home,
and I wished to postpone that as much as possible. Mildred
could never understand my wanderlust and my anxiety over
her never-ending overtures of love and affection and requests
for sexual gratification, which she constantly and at all hours

of the night pressed upon me while I tried to sleep. However, I knew that however late I was, Mildred would probably only raise a token protest in lieu of the fact that I *was* home and could begin once more plunging fruitlessly into the depths of her passion. The only defense available to me was to guzzle quantities of alcoholic beverages that would allow me to arrive home in a state of lethargic consciousness in which a stupor might then be attained.

I did not know what I was going to do with Mildred or how I was ever going to be able to come to a life of harmonious tranquility where matrimonial happiness was a constant joy. The only good thing about it was it gave me a subject of regular worry that I was able to slide endlessly back and forth in my mind during my various ruminations and ramblings over blacktopped back roads. We were not social people and were never invited to parties, nor did we give parties where we invited people to them. We basically lived alone with each other on ten acres of land that was badly eroded in a house of poor quality. I was not drunk but I did not feel sober. The needle on my gas gauge was pointing toward E and had been pointing that way for quite a while. There did not seem to be anything else to do but return home and face the prospect of burying my dog/dealing with my wife. I could see her face just as well and her small ears, and I could see kissing her nose and her chin and her cheeks and the small hollow place inside her soft little elbow, and I felt like disaster was on the way, since it felt like one of those evenings that I'd already had too many of. I wanted to do all I could for her, but it didn't seem like I could do anything for her at all.

Upon entering my yard, I saw there were no lights on at my house and my dog was lying just as I had left him. Mildred's car was not in the carport, which was a most unusual sight. I was not extremely steady entering my house but stumbled around only a bit before I found the light switch and turned it on. There on the coffee table, held down by an empty beer bottle, was a note that was addressed to me. It said:

Dear Leroy,
I have met another man and I have gone away with him.
He has the equipment to take care of my problem and we
have already "roadtested" it, so to speak. Forgive me, my
darling, but he is the one man I have been searching for
all my adult life. I have taken the cats but of our house
and property I want nothing. My attorney will be in con-
tact with you but as for me I must bid you adieu and wish
for you that you will some day find your own happiness.

XXX,
Mildred

It took a while for the words to sink in, for the reality of what I was reading to hit me. Mildred was gone, apparently, with another man with a huge penis. The reality sobered me up some, so I went out to my truck and got another beer and walked back over to my dog. He was still there, still dead, only by then he had begun to stiffen a little as rigor mortis set in. I knew I needed to get a shovel and bury him but I decided it could wait until morning. I looked at my house and I could feel the emptiness of it already. I went up on the porch and sat down. I could imagine Mildred in a hotel room some-where with the man she had taken, and I could imagine them moving together and Mildred's happiness and total fulfillment and joy with her newfound sexual gratification. I hated that I had never been able to give her what she wanted. I knew that I would just have to try and find another wife. I didn't know where to start looking, but I decided that I would start first thing in the morning, as soon as the dog had been given a suitable burial. There were plenty of women out there, and I knew that somewhere there was one that was right for me. I hoped when I found her, I would know it. I felt like one part of my life was over but that another, just as important part, was beginning. I felt a lot of optimism, and I knew I could get another dog. But I was already beginning to feel a little lone-some, and I could feel it surrounding the house, closing in. I tried not to think about it, but I sat out there on the porch for a long time that night, doing just that. I looked around for the cats, but it was true, she had taken every last one, looked like. It would have been nice to have had maybe just one, a small one, to sit and pet and listen to it purr. I knew they could be cruel and vicious, but I knew they needed love also just like everyone else. I thought about Mildred in that other man's arms, and how fine she looked in a bathing suit. Right about then I started missing her, and the loneliness I have been speaking of really started to set in.

Gold Nuggets

It was a bar somewhere between Orange Grove and Pascagoula, one of those places where they charge you nothing to get in and then five dollars for a ten-ounce Schlitz. It was dark. Everybody had on sunglasses but me. My friend had gone off and I didn't know what had happened to him. I knew what I was, though, and I was trying to learn to live with it. I thought if I could just make it through the night, that everything would be sort of okay when the sun came up.

This place sold nude dancing. Just Ts, no As. I said, Well, bring on the dancing girls. I knew I was suffering from alcohol poisoning, and that it had settled in my brain. I could drink one beer and I'd start thinking differently, about everything. This little girl who had not even graduated from high school pranced out on the stage waving a scarf around her head and stumbling in her high heels. Her poor little titties were about a 32A.

And then like sharks two women glided in on each side of me. The one on the left had dark hair in her armpits. Tremendous titties. I checked them out and drank half of my ten ounces, then eyed the right flank. Blonde, maybe pregnant. Already stroking the inside of my thigh.

Oooooooh. Ooo and ooo and ooo. She scratched the head of it like a mosquito bite. She turned her head and yawned and came back beaming. They had nude paintings on the walls, sort of a celebration of sex, which I certainly had nothing against if I could just celebrate a little of it myself.

The little chickadee up on the stage was bent over in my face, revealing all her secrets, but I figured this kid already had two kids of her own at home and a babysitter waiting for her to show up. It made me feel slightly perverted.

"Why don't you buy me a drank?" the one on the left said. "I'd love to have a drank."

I fumbled around for my money. She helped me peel off three ones and raised her hand. They hadn't even set it on the table when the other one leaned over and said she wanted one, too. So I bought her one. And told her to bring me another beer. I didn't care. I wanted to wake up broke and sober. I figured if I couldn't buy a drink, I couldn't get a drink. We jawed some old shit, it didn't matter what we said. We all knew the score. Their job was to rob me, my job was to pay for the robbery. All night long if possible.

I picked up the blonde's drink and tasted it when she wasn't looking. Grape Kool-Aid. Well, I thought, I don't have to put up with this shit. She got up and took her drink with her and, I don't know, poured it out or something, then came back all friendly wanting another one.

I'd gotten surly and terse. I was feeling mean. I'd had about all their shit I wanted to take. I figured there were some big dark mean motherfuckers waiting back in the shadows to break my head and roll me when I went to the bathroom. The little beaverette up on the stage had gotten down on her hands, legs spread, pumping that thing up and down. And I just shook my head.

Blonde, she leaned over, sort of stroked my neck.

"You gonna buy me another drank?" she said.

"Buy your own damn drink."

She looked offended. "Well, honey, if you don't buy me another one I'll have to get up and go."

I told her not to let the door hit her in the ass. Of course she got all huffy and left. Then I turned on the other one.

"And you," I said. "You can just get your ass up and go, too. Fucking grape Kool-Aid. You want me to tell you what you can do with your grape Kool-Aid?"

She didn't say anything. She just looked away, and immediately I felt like an asshole. Sometimes I feel like an asshole about ten times a day. But I didn't want to be hustled. There I was, all the way off down on the coast, didn't know how I was going to get back, my friend had gone, and I had less than I'd started out with. Shrimp money. People depending on me, already buying their crab boil and their cocktail sauce. So there was only so much leeway I had. Maybe I could haggle the guy at the boat down, maybe I couldn't. If I spent their money and then couldn't haggle, I was up Shit Creek. But at that point I wouldn't have minded legging down.

In dark places you can't see much. But on the side of this girl's face sitting next to me I saw something shining down her cheek. And I thought, Well, you asshole, you messed up again.

"Shit," I said. "I'm sorry."

She looked around and tried to smile. "It's okay," she said.

"I didn't mean to be rude to you," I said.

"It's okay."

But it wasn't okay. I knew it wasn't okay and she knew it wasn't okay. Here she hadn't done anything but ask for a three-dollar drink of Kool-Aid and I'd tried to run her off.

"Let me buy you a beer," I told her.

"I can't drink a beer."

"What? You don't like beer? You got some medical problem?"

"Oh no. I like beer fine. I'd love a beer."

"Well, hell," I said. "Then drink one."

She got sort of close to me then. She leaned over to my ear, so I could look right down that Big Valley.

"They don't 'low it," she said.

"Don't 'low what?"

She jerked her head. "You know."

I looked in that direction. Then I saw the mean-ass momma watching us. Black chick, about thirty, medium fro, teeth probably filed to tiny points. Definitely not a vegetarian.

"Listen," I said. "If I want to buy you a beer, can't I buy you a beer?"

"Well, I don't know," she said. "They don't like for us to drink."

She smelled sort of bad. I was crazy and I knew it. Maybe her husband—if she had one—she probably did—was a shrimper and she shrimped with him in the daytime. Maybe she'd been down in the hot hold all day long shoveling up shrimp with a shovel. I didn't care about any of that. She was a human being. She had the right to drink a beer. Even a drunk knows that.

"Just wait a minute," I said. I got up from the table and staggered over to the momma. A hard chick. You could tell it from her eyes. No telling what she'd seen or done in her life. I wouldn't have wanted to fistfight her. She could have been pretty and might have been at one time. No more, though. All she was after was money. Money to get the hell away from that dive she'd found herself in.

"Listen," I said. "I want to buy this girl over here a beer. Do you care?"

She turned a cold pair of eyes on me. Eyes that cut me to my soul. They went up and down me, and stopped on my face. How many had she seen like me? I'd never seen such contempt.

"We don't 'low it," she said, nearly whispering. But then she leaned over. "But you can buy *me* a drink if you want to, sugar."

She didn't look bad. She had some huge ones. All I had was shrimp money. I could see the sunshine coming down on my head the next morning while I was trying to find the *Elvira Mulla* or the *Vulla Elmirea* or the *Meara Vulmira* or the *WhatEverItWas*. There had just been whispered, hurried conversations over the phone, and I didn't even like the people involved. What if the nets had holes in them or the shrimp weren't sleeping?

Well, this chick wasn't bad. She was hard. But I could see that she could be soft. Money softened her. She'd smelled money on me and right away she'd softened. Maybe she'd take me home. I didn't know. But I was so damn lonely, and horny, that I was willing to take a chance on almost anything. Plus, I was drunk.

For a minute there I sort of got the big picture. You back off from anything and get the big picture, you can figure out almost anything if you figure on it long enough. I looked at myself and I thought: Now listen, you got all this money belongs to all these people and you're supposed to take care of it. Now what the hell's gonna happen if you show up without the money or the shrimp either one? What if you just blow all the money, and don't buy the shrimp, and go back home to all those people who've already bought their crab boil and crackers and cocktail sauce? Well, you're gonna have some people pissed at you, that's what.

But, now, think about them. Think about Ed, that son of a bitch, think about him in the first place. Did that son of a bitch ask you if you wanted some shrimp last year when he went off to Pensacola and went deep-sea fishing and didn't catch shit? When he puked in a bar that Milos López once actually got thrown out of? Did that s.o.b. ask you if you wanted him to bring you some shrimp? Hell naw. Fuck *him*.

And who's the other one? Ted. That fucking Ted. That bastard. You ought to whip his ass just on general principle. Son of a bitch. Did he ever invite you over to his private bass lake when they were jerking those ten-pound lunkers out of there? Hell naw. The son of a bitch even called the law on some kids.

Now I had to consider all that stuff. I couldn't deal very well with it. She was smiling in my face and I had all that money in my pocket and I wasn't too fond of these fuckers who'd sent me down there to the Gulf to get all their shrimp for them. And all I was trying to do originally was buy a beer for a girl who shook her ass naked in a dark bar where dark people like me stalked their lusts.

"She can't drink a beer," this chick said.

"Why?" I said. "Listen, goddamnit, I'm getting pissed off at the way y'all treat these girls. What? Y'all own em?"

"Yeah, that's right," she said. "We own em. They dumb enough to come in here and work, we own em. Buy em and sell em if we get ready to."

She gave me a look so hard I said: "Wait a minute. You ain't that hard, are you? You ain't that bad, are you? Why don't you let her have a beer? What's it going to hurt?"

"It's against the rules."

"What rules?" I said. "Who makes up the rules?" I leaned over close to her and said softly: "Have you ever questioned the rules?"

"You so hot to take somebody out, why don't you take me out?" she said.

What? And maybe get my throat cut? (An anecdote to testify to this madness: The night before, I got pissed off at my friend because he was drunk and I wasn't and I was ready to go and he wasn't, I begged him five or six times too but he wouldn't hear it, he was jumping hot with this beavette, so I split. Right down the beach to our hotel room. I thought it was only a block and it was like four miles. I had to sit down and rest a few times, and I found out something. At night, that tide goes out. There's no water there. And you wouldn't believe the nasty shit that's lying down there. I mean, dead rotten fish, and Coke cups and stuff, and it doesn't look at all nice with that moonlight pouring down over that slimy sand. And I found out later that it had only been a week before when some guy got his throat cut down there, from ear to ear, on the beach, at night, late like that, probably in the same exact spot I was sitting in. Boy.) But boy I'd wanted me some of this for quite a while, just like every other white man. I almost did a double-flip hotswoon.

"Come on, baby," she said. "Take a little ride wit me."

I followed her out the door, the back door, where black guys were muttering in the dark and I couldn't tell if they were shucking oysters or not. She had it parked behind the Dumpster, where the lights didn't shine. When we walked up to that machine, it did. Brand new Henweigh, red, magnesiums on all four sides; she had the Alpine Stereo System. I was almost scared to get in the car with her. But I did.

"I got some cold cognac if you'd like some, baby," she said, when she had the little jewel purring like a kitten at its mama's titty. She sort of ran her hands up her legs and pulled the dress back.

"Hold on," she said, and I turned the cognac straight up. Brought it down immediately, wheezing and gasping and coughing, damn near choking to death. She rammed it out of the parking lot and hit second and squealed viciously on the corners until she hit a straightaway and we must have been doing seventy by then and she downshifted and braked sharply and whipped it around a curve and out onto the street, and then two streets over she pulled in behind a bread truck, and four big black guys jumped out with knives and guns and robbed my terrified ass while she hung out the window on her elbow laughing herself silly, the pee running down her leg, maybe, I guess, saying, Hoo boy, you white boys something else.

Well, it scared the shit out of me, naturally. I felt weak all over for about twelve minutes. But then I got to thinking about it and said to myself, Well, it's gone now, wasn't anything you could do, you still got your hotel room, you can charge some beer on your MasterCard and haul ass in the morning before they check. That and plus I had five one hundred dollar bills folded into a minute thing in the heel of my right sock. I'd just tell my groovy employers that they'd stripped me naked, even looked up my ass. Real killers. So I started walking back up the beach. I'd sobered up a little, what with the robbery and all. I didn't know how I'd get back into North Mississippi and my beloved pine trees. They'd specifically stated that they wanted headless shrimp. Like Captain Mike McDonald and his crew were going to sit back and shuck the fuckers. But that was just the kind of rich ignorance I was dealing with. I wanted to go out on the boat with them. I wanted to pull the nets. I wanted to see what came up from the ocean depths, what unspeakable stuff spilled out when they hoisted it up onto the deck.

But the Gold Nugget beckoned. I could see it from the beach, from the dark water, from the sucking tide sucking further south with each suck. I had to sit down to get out my money. It was good money.

A whole new shift had come one. I settled at a table, my hands trembling just a little. I knew the sister was going to come back a little later, and I didn't know what to do about it. My ass was in a crack. I tried to figure out how much they had taken off me. It was somewhere around three hundred dollars. I had two hundred dollars' worth of coolers in my pickup.

The women were still dancing, except that the junior high shift had come on. I was really starting to feel like a degenerate, and sick with what it all finally came down to. Getting robbed is kind of like getting your ass whipped, in that somebody else has beaten you. It doesn't matter that he's got a gun or a knife, you could have had a gun or a knife too and fought for your money. I decided to go armed from then on, just as soon as I could afford a gun or a knife.

I was wobbling at my table a little. I knew people could probably see it. I hated that, sort of, didn't want to be drunk in public, but didn't know what to do about it right then. There wasn't anything would fix it but another drink. I summoned somebody and somebody brought one. I was getting eyes from the bar again.

I didn't want to mess with any more of those girls. I'd already seen the fine ones, up in Memphis, where they let them go naked in front of you and then expect you to behave yourself. I knew in some men that kind of stuff caused rapes, which is why it was dangerous to offer that kind of stuff to the general public, since a lot of times the general public had a hard dick and little conscience. I decided to just sit there and nurse my beer, lick my wounds, and see if the chick walked back in.

There were guys groping chicks in the corners. I didn't know what the hour of night was. Late was all I knew. My friend wasn't anywhere around. He knew the name of the boat and I didn't. He knew the dock they docked at. But he'd probably already had his throat cut and was being eaten by fish, or the dogs and cats at the seafood plants. It didn't make me just real happy or at ease sitting there waiting for him. Maybe he'd given up on ever finding me and had just gone back home. That'd be real hucky ducky if that was the case. If he'd taken my pickup that'd be real uncool and I'd have to catch the big Hound going north emptyhanded. Rich fuckers like they were, they could get things done. They might even hire my legs broken. I knew they knew plenty of people they could sub it out to.

I ordered another beer. Some waitress brought it and I gave her some money. She popped her gum and gave me my change. I lit a smoke. Just then I noticed a guy sitting near me, almost at my elbow. He looked sort of hungry. I glanced at him, and then I didn't pay any more attention to him. All I wanted to do was just drink until something happened. I knew if I drank long enough, it would.

I got a little philosophical sitting there, surrounded by all that sin, feeling so mired down in it. I hadn't been raised to go into places like that. And there I was in one. I didn't know where the sun might find me. I just hoped it wasn't a place as dark as that one.

That guy leaned over and groped my leg. I sighed.

I'd had to deal with a thing like that once before. It had been a long time ago and I'd nearly forgotten it. A sailor had bought me a drink and then touched me in an unwelcome way in a bar. I thanked the sailor for the drink and told him to get his hand off my leg. He removed it and said he didn't mean anything by it. Then he told me about his wife and family and friends for twenty minutes. Then he bought me another drink. Then he put his hand on me in an unwelcome way again. I remember sighing inwardly. I leaned over to the bartender and told him I hated to get thrown out of the bar, but if that guy put his hand on me again in an unwelcome way again I was going to have to knock the shit out of him. Then I told the sailor exactly the same words. It made him hot, and words were said, and I wound up choking him. It hadn't been nice, and I knew this thing probably wasn't going to be nice either.

I turned around and looked at this guy. He had a cap shoved back on his head, and some missing teeth, and a black eye. His hand on my leg felt like a granite claw. I looked into his eyes. They were tinged with yellow and red, and they looked a little wobbly.

He was a real big guy.

I sat there and held my beer, wondering what to do. For all I knew he could have been a henchman, one of hers. I knew to operate like she did she had to have henchmen.

I finally told him he wouldn't believe how much I'd appreciate the shit out of it if he'd get his hand off my leg.

I thought Yeah, their goddamn shrimp. Their damn shrimpy minds. Why do you want to put yourself in the employ of people like that? Who have no interest in you other than what you can do for them? I was really getting sleepy and I yawned several times. It didn't look like my friend was going to show up and I knew somebody had to go down to the dock the next morning and try to find that boat. And not just any boat. *That* boat, where they were selling them for $1.35 a pound medium jumbo, cutting out the middleman and passing the savings on to the consumer. I decided I'd be best off booking for the local hotel, so that's what I did, like a fat man's ass.

It was hot as hell in the parking lot the next morning. Some firemen were having a convention in the Holiday Inn, and they had ladder trucks set up in the parking lot, and they were giving rides to the general public. Since I was general public, I got on one. I had the fear of maybe getting up there and puking down on somebody a hundred feet below. But it was really impressive up there above the roof of the Holiday Inn. For one thing, you could see all those shrimp boats out there in the water running their nets. The sun was shining, but the sky looked smoky. It looked like they were just dredging ton after ton of little shrimps up. It made me feel a whole lot better, looking out over all that industry. I sort of got the big picture sitting up there and realized how small and unimportant my quest was, in light of the tons of available seafood already destined for restaurants all over the South. I decided to just find a shrimp boat docked with a fresh load, jew them down as much as I could, load up and haul ass.

I had a little difficulty manipulating in the traffic. There were two lanes going seventy miles per hour and the white sand beaches were loaded with women in bikinis. I wondered if any of the little beaverettes from the Gold Nugget were out there sunning but then realized they were probably in American History class reading about Benjamin Franklin. I wondered what he would have thought about all that shit, women running around nearly naked and all. I passed the Gold Nugget, which was on the ocean side of the road. It looked deserted, empty, boarded up. It was only eleven a.m., though. I started to pull in and then I said Naaaaaaa. I went on down the road until I got to the harbor, where gulls were flying, and masts were sticking up everywhere. I parked as close as I could and got out. The sun was burning down, and the beer started running out of me. I didn't know how many I'd had the night before. It must have been some kind of ungodly amount, judging from the stuff that was pouring out of me. I couldn't hardly see for the sweat in my eyes.

I started walking down the dock, checking everything out. I didn't know which section I was in. I knew I had to get to the right section, but I didn't know if I was in it or not. There were some neat sportfishermen lined up smartly along the dock with names like *Judy* and *Becca* and *Mama's Dinghy*. I kept walking and looking.

I was wanting a cold beer. I could feel the weight of all that expectation on me. I knew something bad must have happened to my friend, and I didn't feel real good about it. I didn't know how I'd be able to explain it to his wife and all. It had all started out so innocently anyway. We were just going to go down there and goof off a few days, make a shrimp run. Be back at work on Monday. There it was Monday and I didn't have shit to show for it. I knew they'd can me. The job I had wasn't worth a damn anyway, just putting washers in little holes. It wasn't anything that made me feel real fulfilled.

I was lost, and people could tell it. There were people with caps on, and old women weighing plastic baskets of shrimp, and other people with tanned skins and sunglasses watching me stumble around on the dock. Millionaires, probably, some of them, up from Orlando or Jacksonville or Destin, just taking a week off. I kept walking, and was grateful for my own shades. If the eyes were the mirror to the soul, I didn't want anybody to see inside mine. I kept walking. I knew all this was just a temporary setback. It didn't mean that I couldn't ever be saved from my life, or that I'd never find the boat I was looking for. Somewhere, somewhere there, was a connection I could make, and I knew that all I had to do was stay out there until I found it.

I staggered on down the dock, looking, sweating, among browned women in the sun, diamonds glinting, doing all I could at the time, knowing the sun would always go down, and another night would come, that our forms of salvation were ours to choose, as blessed to the misguided like me as any church.

Waiting for the Ladies

My wife came home crying from the Dumpsters, said there was some pervert over there jerked down his pants and showed her his schlong. I asked her how long this particular pecker was—I was drinking beer, not taking it half seriously—and she said it sort of resembled a half-grown snail, or slug, she said, a little hairy. It was so *disgusting*, she said, and gave off this little shiver, doing her shoulders the way she does.

Well, a sudden unreasonable anger suddenly came over me, and I slammed my beer down. I'd already slammed several down. I said by God I'd go take care of the son of a bitch. I said, If it ain't safe for women and kids to walk the roads, what'll you think'll happen when lawlessness takes over, and crime sets in, and the sick and the sexually deviated can sling their penises out in front of what might be some little kid the next time? She was just too tore up to talk about it any more. Had to go lay down and hold one forearm over her eyes. That sort of made me mad. This unknown guy getting his own personal tiny rocks off had messed up my own sexual gratification, and besides that, by God, it just wasn't right. Here I was a working man, or had been, and come to find out it ain't even safe to lay over here in your own bed and let your wife take the garbage off.

I didn't figure I'd need no gun or anything, but I did take my beer. I figured since he'd already dropped his drawers he'd be done hit the bushes, and I thought I could ride around some and listen to country music songs about drinking and cheating and losing love and finding it, since it looked like I wasn't going to be pumping any red-hot baby batter into my own favorite womb any time soon.

Riding over there, I thought about the injustice of how a few people could fuck up everything. I'd heard about these people sucking toes and stuff. I didn't want it around me. I even devised a plan. I left out a few details early on there but my wife had gone on to say that she'd seen this guy sitting there in his pickup before, when she'd been going down the road to some other place, just sitting there, not dumping any garbage or anything. Waiting on his next victim, I supposed, some innocent person he could terrorize. I said well I'd just start keeping my shotgun in my truck and ride over that way about every day, and the next time I saw that pickup (she said it was a blue Ford) I'd just stop and haul it out and peck up his paintjob a little bit until he decided to get his ass back to wherever he came from in the first place.

I got over there and of course there was nothing there. Just a bunch of trash and garbage on the ground right in front of the Dumpsters, and treetops people had dropped off, and wet magazines on the ground, and a little thin sad puppy scared of me somebody'd dropped off, so hungry he couldn't decide whether to stay or run. A son of a bitch who'll drop his pants in front of some woman he's not familiar with is the same kind of son of a bitch'll drop off a puppy like that, thinking somebody'll give him a good home. Good home, my ass. Some of these Vietnamese around here'll eat him.

I didn't know how far this perversion thing had spread, how much word of it had got around. I didn't want to sit there in my pickup thinking people driving by had already heard of the pervert and might think I was him. I tried to call up that puppy. I got down on my heels and clicked and whistled and snapped my fingers and talked nice to him, but all he'd do was roll over with his legs up in the air and his tail between his legs, peeing on himself in little spurts. Somebody had ruined him, beat him, stomped him, him roughly the age of an eighteen-month-old baby, in dog years. I knew some Humaner would come by and capture him and take him to the pound. I should have gone on and killed him. How would the gas be any better than a knock in the head to him? That might've been Napoleon Bonaparte reincarnated running around there, sniffing coffee grounds.

I took off down the road there and rode around a while. What would have to be wrong with a guy to make him flang his thang out in front of women? It had to be some kind of guy who couldn't get any pussy, was too messed up in some way to get some from anybody, even for money, wanted some bad, and had developed this overpowering urge to gratificate himself, ergo, like the mirror is to the image, himself twinned in their eyes, what he imagined to be his big penis, his brutal, killing penis, swinging like a nine-pound hammer, suspended out there for all womanhood to draw back and gasp from, which, in his opinion, was what was happening.

I felt sort of bad for the guy. I didn't know if I needed to go talk to Daddy about it or not. I figured the guy was hollow-eyed, sat in a dark room with his mother watching TV all day long, eating popcorn, and waited for late evening before he started stalking his lusts. I was beginning to get a pretty good mental picture of him already. He was about fifty, with wattley skin around his neck, shaky hands, maybe a dirty cap pulled down low over his eyes and white stubbly whiskers on his jaws, weak chin, bad shoes, one of those belts about ten inches too long for him with the excess hanging loose. Yeah, he was starting to form up in my mind. He was a wimpy sumbitch from back yonder. His had not been an easy life, and he might not have all his mental faculties. He might stand in line at the welfare office every Wednesday, holding his mother's hand, and she might have cared for him like this since he was a baby. She might've had bad love, or love run off, or he might've been in the womb too long. They had some little awful house way back up in the woods around London Hill or somewhere, with tin cans out in the yard and mud on the porch, and bleak was a word they didn't understand, since that was the world as they knew it. She didn't know why he took off like that in the evenings sometimes, and she'd never recognized that he might have secret needs he was too scared to tell anybody about, or maybe she didn't even think about stuff like that.

I made one long slow circle through Potlockney and DeLay and came back up through the Crocker Woods, cut through to Paris and back through the Webb Graveyard Road, but I didn't see a blue Ford pickup parked anywhere. I knew he was back home by then, sitting on the floor in a dark room right in front of the television, his eyes blank, his hand cramming popcorn in his mouth, the lights of the "Bill Cosby Show" flickering across his face, his mother asleep on the couch behind him, unaware of the twisted needs in him, a mindless drooling idiot, someone without enough sense to turn the television off, chewing, thinking about my wife, where to try it tomorrow, a motherfucker you could crush.

Later on that night I wound up at Daddy's, drunk, as usual, when I went over there, him laying up there all by himself waiting for me, patient, never looking when you walked in like he was even expecting company. We never argued any. I always told him something or asked him something and he gave me some advice and I took it. It wasn't any different this time.

He turned his old flat gray eyes over to me real slow, his eyes as gray as his flattop, smoking one Camel after another on that old Army cot twenty years after the doctors told him lung cancer had killed him, a glass of whiskey nearby, Humphrey Bogart on the TV. *The Caine Mutiny.* One of his favorites. Laying there in his long underwear without a shave in a week, indomitable, old boxer, warrior, lover, father.

I told him somebody'd showed his dick to my wife.

He wanted to know how big a dick it was.

I told him she said it was just a small one. He paused. We watched Humphrey measure out some sand with a spoon. I felt almost out of control.

Then he looked back around to me, swung his old flat gray eyes up there on my face and said, Son, a little dick's sorta like a Volkswagen. It's all right around the house but you don't want to get out on the road with it. I didn't know what to say. He told me to bring him some whiskey sometime. I left soon after.

I'd quit my job after sixteen years and drawn that state retirement money out, way over ten thousand dollars. Back in those days I thought that money would last forever. I was just laying around the house drinking beer, poking Dorothea soon as she walked in the door. I did the same thing the guy at the Dumpsters did, only behind closed doors. I had a woman who looked good, who liked to wear a garter belt and black stockings and keep the light on.

But that insult to her wore on me. I'd get in the truck to ride around and I'd get to thinking about it. I'd get to thinking about the humiliation she felt when that guy did that. I even called the sheriff's department one day and reported it, and talked to a deputy about it. They knew who it was, and I like to fell over. They knew his name. They told me his name. I said Well, if this sick son of a bitch is running around out here jerking his pants down in front of people, why in the hell don't y'all do something about it? They said he was harmless, that he'd already been arrested six times for doing it, twice in front of Kroger's uptown when ladies tried to load up their groceries. I said, You think a son of a bitch like that is harmless? They said, Believe me, he's harmless. They said, Believe me, there's a lot worse than that going on that you don't know nothing about. They said, If you did know what all was going on, you wouldn't sleep at night.

That made me uneasy and I decided to get in my truck and ride around some more. That retirement money was stacked up inside that bank account drawing 6.5 percent interest. I had beer and cigarettes unlimited. Dorothea had gotten that promotion and her boss liked her, took her out to lunch so she wouldn't have to spend her own money. She had a real future in head of her.

I put my gun in the truck. Squirrel season was open, and that meant rabbit, too, and once in a while after dark you'd see the green eyes standing out in the cut fields that meant deer. Hamburger meat was $1.89 a pound. Double-ought buckshot was thirty-three cents. Some nights I was Have Truck, Will Kill, Palladin with a scattergun.

Those nights back then out on those country roads, with that sweet music playing and that beer cold between my legs and an endless supply of cigarettes and the knowledge that Dorothea was waiting back at home with her warm pubic hairs sometimes made me prolong the sheer pleasure of getting back to it, just riding around thinking about how good it was going to be when I got back. And then there was a little son of a bitch who didn't have any, who'd never know what it was like or the heat that was in it, like a glove that fit you like a fist but better, warmer, wetter, no wonder he wanted some so bad it drove him to have one-way sex with strangers. Dorothea hadn't said, but since she'd commented on the size of it, I figured his pud was down when he did it, not up. I wondered what he'd have done if some woman had walked over and slapped the shit out of him.

I puzzled over it and puzzled over it and drove for nights on end looking for that blue pickup, but if there was one in the country I didn't see it. I took back roads and side roads and pig trails that buzzards couldn't hardly fly over when it rained, and I decided he'd done decided to take his goobergrabbing on down the road somewhere else. By then I wasn't even mad and just wanted to talk to him, tell him calmly that he couldn't run around doing stuff like that. I was sure by then that he'd been raised without a father, and I could imagine what their lives were like, him and his mother, eating their powdered eggs, and I couldn't imagine how we could spend 1.5 billion dollars on a probe to look at Jupiter and yet couldn't feed and clothe the people in our own country. I wanted a kinder, gentler world like everybody else, but I knew we couldn't get it blasting it all off in space, or not providing for people like him. Who was to say that if he got cleaned up with some fresh duds, a little education, some new Reeboks, he couldn't get a blowjob in Atlanta? Hell. Why not educate? Defumigate? Have changes we could instigate? Why couldn't everybody, the whole country, participate?

Then I saw his truck.

It was backed up between some bushes on the side of the road. A cold feeling washed over me, made me lose all compassion. I said, Here this sick son of a bitch is sitting by the side of the road waiting for some innocent woman like my wife to come along and have car trouble, and instead of helping her change her tire he's going to run out in the road flonging his dong, whipping his mule, and it gave me a bad case of the creeps. I said, I'm fixing to tell this son of a bitch a thing or two. I thought of Boo Radley, how sweet he turned out to be. But I knew this wasn't nothing like that. I went on up to the end of the road and I turned around and came back. My shotgun was loaded. I pulled it over next to me. It was warm, the stock smooth—like Shane said, a tool only as good or as bad as the man who uses it—and I wondered if I could kill that man for what he'd done to my wife.

He'd already pulled out, and you can tell when somebody wants you to pass. They'll slow down, maybe because they're drinking beer and don't want to turn one up in front of you because they don't know if you're the law or not, since all they can see is your headlights. They'll poke along and poke along, waiting for you to pass, slowing down to a crawl in the straightaways, and it's maddening if it's happening to you, if you're riding around wondering why your wife's boss keeps driving by the house and waving out the window, almost as if he's looking to see who's home, if you're riding around wondering if you're riding around a little too much.

I got right on his bumper and rode that busted set of tail-lights and watched that stiff neck and that cap pulled down low over his eyes, that head turning every five seconds to the rearview mirror for eight or nine miles, him crawling, me crawling along behind him, letting him know that somebody was onto his game and following him all the way home. I went all the way down through Yocona bottom behind him, where it's straight for three miles, nothing coming, him speeding up a little, me speeding up, too, thinking: You son of a bitch. Pull your dick out in front of her now. Swing that dick around like a billy club now.

I kept drinking and following him and he started weaving and I did, too, and we almost ran off the road a few times, but I stayed right on his ass until he got down to Twin Bridges and tried to outrun me, stayed right with him or pulled up beside him and then I eased off, thinking he might have a wreck. I didn't want to kill him. I just wanted to talk to him. I kept telling myself that. I kept drinking. Everybody wanted pussy and pussy was good. But this guy had a hell of a way of going after it. I laid in there right on his ass, and when he turned around in George Fenway's driveway, I turned right around with him and followed him almost all the way to Bobo.

I let him get a little ahead of me. I knew where he lived. Deputy sheriff had told me, and his name was on the mailbox. I knew he was trying to run, hide, I knew by then that he knew he was caught somehow. I knew there had to be a whole lot of fear going through his mind, who was after him, what'd they want, all that kind of stuff. He just hadn't thought about any of that when he flicked his Bic.

When I got to where he lived, the truck was behind the house and there wasn't a light on. I coasted by twice with the headlights off. Then I killed it by the side of the road and listened for a while. It was quiet. Some light wires were humming. That was it. Dorothea and her boss had taken some awful long lunches. I got out with the shotgun and a beer and closed the door. The law wasn't there, and I was the law. *Vigilante Justice*. Patrick Swayze and somebody else. *Dirty Dancing*. But he never flashed his trash.

The yard was mud, the house almost dark. I could just see that one little light inside that was Johnny Carson saying goodnight. I knew he might have a gun, and might be scared enough to use it. In my state I thought I could holler self-defense in his front yard.

I hope I didn't ruin their lives.

The door was open, and the knob turned under my hand. The barrel of the gun slanted down from under my arm, and I tracked their mud on their floor. He didn't have his cap on, and his hair wasn't like what I'd imagined. It was gray, but neatly combed, and his mother was sobbing silently on the couch and feeding a pillow into her mouth.

He said one thing, quietly: "Are you fixing to kill us?"

Their eyes got me.

I sat down, asking first if I could. That's when I started telling both of them what my life then was like.

Old Soldiers

for Lisa

I used to spend a lot of time with Mr. Aaron. He had a bench you could pass out on behind the stove and that's where I was one day. We'd been after some antlerless deer that morning, or just whatever happened to run across the road in front of the dogs, but it was so cold their noses couldn't smell anything. We'd resorted to whiskey. It was only one o'clock but I was messed up, I won't deny it. My truck was parked at the store, and they dropped me off there at my request. I told them I'd be okay. They didn't want to leave me, they were my friends, I'd made an impossible shot at 340 yards the day before on a running eight-point buck. We'd already eaten him. I told them to leave me, that I was in good hands.

Mr. Aaron was quietly benevolent. He never said anything. You as a stranger could say hi to him and he'd just grunt. He

91

was my kind of people. I got a small green glass Coke for my whiskey toddy, and I settled on the bench. I had part of a pint in my game bag. Before long he brought around a hot Budweiser and we toasted each other silently. He despised all the needless words that people said. It was his store and he didn't like loudmouths. Our darker brothers he especially turned a deaf ear on. Once I saw a darker woman pull up outside and want her air checked. He checked it. But it took him about thirty minutes. When she left, all four tires were very low.

He had a Mitsubishi TV we were watching with the sound turned off. My boots were thawing out beside the stove and water was puddling on the floor. Mr. Aaron brought a mop and swabbed and never said a word about the mess. He kept his beer in the candy case, hot. If kids came in giving him any shit he ran their asses off. I was almost swooning with delight. I knew he was ready with a war story.

"By God, I miss your daddy," he said.

I was on my back, flat, drink on my belly. I didn't even have to coax him sometimes. It was warm in there and I took off my coat. Here was a man who never turned down a drink of whiskey.

"By God, it was rough, too. Your daddy knowed how it was. I seen him in Germany one time he was riding on a tank with a machine gun in his lap. Stopped the tank and he had a bottle of brandy and we got drunk. Run that tank through some woman's wash line and through a post office. Course that was after the worst fighting was over. In France them French girls run to meet us holding their dresses up, was so glad to see American soldiers instead of German. They was probably not a one of them over twelve years old had not been raped by Germans at one time or another."

I felt like getting the crying jags over my father and him. But the whiskey will make you want to cry after it makes you want to laugh. I could have stayed with that old man forever. He had seventeen hundred silver dollars. He had two cars but he never went anywhere, and he ate Vienna sausage off the shelf. Had done it for thirty years.

"How's your leg?" I said. I always asked him about his leg. Most people who carried on their commerce there didn't even know about his leg. I did. All the shrapnel had gone into the bone where they wouldn't cut for it. There was a perfect circle of scar tissue on his calf that looked to me like a grenade ring.

He waved the question away with his hand. "It's all right," he said. "They'd might near have to cut my whole leg off to get rid of it. It's pitiful what the world's going to now."

Somebody stopped beside the gas pump and waited five minutes for him to come out.

"I ain't getting up again," he said, then got up immediately for another beer from the candy case. He brought me back a pack of pigskins and threw them in my lap. The car pulled away.

"Damn niggers," he said. "Think you ought to wait on em hand and foot. But you look at all this shit. Reason the government ain't got no money right now is cause they shooting it all up in space. What damn good's it do to beat the Russians to the moon? I ain't going to the moon. Ain't nobody in his right mind would even want to go to the moon. I don't even think they been up there. I think they just took a buncha pictures over in Africa or somewhere."

I was standing outside the Kream Kup in Oxford the Sunday afternoon Neil Armstrong walked on the moon. We all looked up there. That was before I'd ever had any nooky. But by that afternoon in Mr. Aaron's store, I'd had plenty.

I must have fallen asleep. There was a long period when nothing was said. I tried to raise up and I couldn't raise up. I heard a rhythmic noise. The front door was shut and the lights were off. In my socked feet I could sneak. From behind the curtain behind the counter came the rhythmic noises. They stopped. I peeked.

Mr. Aaron was pulling a big one out of a lady who lived down the road. It looked like he might have hurt her with it the way she was taking on. I was back on the bench conked seemingly out when Miss Gladys Watson came through adjusting her white Dixie Delite uniform. Soon as the door slammed shut I raised up and said: "Who's that?"

Let me tell you something else Mr. Aaron did one time. He had this old dog named Bobo, whose whole body was crooked from being run over so many times. Mr. Aaron fed him potato chips. He'd go out once a day and dump a bag of pigskins or something on the ground and then go back in. As children we'd all sit around in front of the store, on upended Coke cases and such, and wait for a dogfight to occur. This was in the days before pit bulls, when a dog could get his ass whipped and just go on home. One day Mr. Mavis Edwards, an old man who lived across the road, had been sitting

out there with us. But then he went off to the post office
to get his mail and left a whole pound of baloney on top
of a Coke case. Bobo grabbed it. And was chomping on it
when Mr. Mavis came back. Mr. Mavis had been in the war,
too, the First World War. He carried a cane and wore a Fu
Manchu of snuff spittle. Of course he was incensed. Went
to whipping Bobo about the ears and head with his cane.
But you could see that the dog was ready to kill for that
comparatively juicy snack. I mean, after a steady diet of
potato chips, he was eating the waxed paper along with the
baloney. Mr. Aaron heard the commotion going on outside.
Some other people were fixing flats. The bros who had pulled
up beside the gas pumps were afraid Mr. Aaron would shoot
them if they tried to pump their own. And we didn't know
but what Mr. Aaron might out with his 9MM and burn Mr.
Mavis down. Mr. Mavis had sprayed everybody with snuff
juice during his exhortations. Mr. Aaron came back to the
door and thrust another paper sack at him. "Here!" he said to
Mr. Mavis. Then he reared back and kicked the hell out of
the dog.

Mr. Mavis took the new baloney and said, "Why, hell,
Aaron." He never darkened the door again.

One time I was up at the store after doing my tour in the
service. He always had a soft spot in his heart for the men
who toted the guns. I was going to town and asked him if he
wanted me to bring him anything back and he said yes, whiskey. I bought it and returned. Miss Gladys came in, ostensi-
bly to buy some flour, and fumblefucked around on the shelves

for five minutes after she saw me sitting there. She left in a huff without making a purchase.

He came around there where I was and sat down beside me.

"Listen," he said. "Don't be like me. Get old and you won't have nobody to take care of you."

"Did you not ever want to get married?" I said.

"Nah, hell, wasn't that. They's all married off when I got back."

I knew better. War had hurt him. He never got the bullets and the bombs out of his head. I know he shot men. He once saw a dogfight over the African desert, with all the action at five thousand feet. He said the American plane that went down left a solid black trail of smoke all the way to the ground, and the whole company sat down in the sand and cried. Then they went out that night and killed a bunch of people. He told me that.

He was drunk by the time he'd told it, and that time I left him asleep on the floor. I locked the door before I left. He wouldn't have let me help him across the road to his house.

The other thing I'm fixing to tell you has a lot to do with what I just told you.

This was years later. Uptown in a bar one night. It was raining so hard I had to make a mad dash from my car to the door, raining so hard you could hardly see how to drive with the wipers going full speed. But I got in there and took my coat off and was glad to be in out of the rain. I was between women, living alone for a while again, and I didn't know how or when I'd find another one. The beer I ordered came and I paid.

There was nothing much going on. A few guys shooting pool and a few older women sitting at tables talking. Then I saw Squirrel at about the same time he saw me. I could tell he was drunk. He got up and started making his way over to me. I sat there and waited for him.

He's a good man. He's worked hard all his life laying brick, but he's had his troubles with the bottle. He's somewhere in his fifties, maybe sixties, I don't know now.

He sat down beside me and we talked for a while. Or he did. With drunks you know you just mostly agree and nod your head a lot. You don't have to worry about carrying the conversation, they'll do it. Squirrel was pissed off. He was ready to go home and he didn't have any wheels, because he'd left his wheels at home and come to town with two of the old guys shooting pool. He was ready to go and they weren't. I didn't want to think about what he was working his way up to. I was in out of that rain, I wanted to stay in out of it for a while.

This boy I knew walked in and asked me what in the hell I was doing in there when they had nickel beer up at Abbey's Irish Rose from 7:30 to 9:30 after you paid a two-dollar cover charge upstairs. I told him I didn't know anything about it. Squirrel leaned over right fast and in close to me and said, "Can you take me home?"

There it is a lot of times. You go out somewhere, just planning on drinking a few beers, and you run into some drunk you've known all your life who doesn't have a way home. You either have to take him home, refuse to, or tell him a lie. Usually I tell a lie. I told Squirrel I wasn't planning on going on home for a while, which was the truth. He said he understood and wouldn't think of imposing on me. I felt guilty, and I hated for him to make me feel guilty, but I hadn't brought him up there and poured any whiskey down him. And he lived way back up in the woods on a mud road the mailman has to use a Jeep on when it rains. In four-wheel drive. With Buckshot Mudders.

I finished my first beer and got another one, and Squirrel bummed a cigarette off me. I lit it for him, and he started telling me how he'd lost all his money. I wasn't listening that close, but it was something about them driving down to Batesville and unloading some two-by-fours and him asking the man he was working for to loan him a hundred dollars. The guy gave him five twenties, and when they got back to town, Squirrel paid for two fifths of whiskey. I know they were drinking when they went down there, he didn't have to tell me that. He said that left him about eighty dollars, but he said he didn't have it now and it was making him sick. And he wanted to go home.

"Sumbitches drug me off up here and got me drunk and now they don't want to go home," was what he said.

I hated to hear of his troubles, but I didn't want to drive him all the way back to Old Dallas on those muddy roads in my Chevelle and more than likely slide off into a ditch. He said he wouldn't think of imposing on me. His head was starting to droop. And I was wishing I'd never gone in there. There was no way I could leave without him. He only lived six miles from me.

I always think I'm going to find something when I go out at

night, I don't know why. I always think that, and I never do. I always think I'll find a woman. But if you go out in sadness, that's all you're going to find. It was too quiet in there with him sitting next to me drooping his head, so I got up and put some change into the jukebox. I just had sat down and picked up my beer again when he leaned over and said, "Take me home, Leo. Please, please."

There wasn't anything else I could do. I couldn't sit there and drink beer with gas in my tank and him saying please to me. All he wanted was to get home and get up the next morning in time to go to work. I knew the other guys would stay until last call, and I knew they had his money. I stared at them but they wouldn't even look at us. I picked up my coat and put it on and I led him to the door. I had to help him down the stairs so he wouldn't fall, and then I had to help him into the car. I had some beer on the back seat, and I gave him one after we got up on the bypass.

Squirrel always talked through his nose. I guess he had a birth defect, a partial palate or something like that, but it wasn't hard to understand him. I think it was easier to understand him when he was drunk. I guess he talked slower then. I know I do.

"How many times you ever seen me drunk, Leo?" he said.

"I don't know, Squirrel. Not many."

"You ain't never seen me drunk, have you?"

"Not too many times," I said. "I think I saw you drunk about six months ago, out there one night."

"How bout opening this beer for me? I can't get this doddamn thing open."

I opened the beer for him and then gave him another cigarette. It was still raining and I was dreading that drive up that
muddy road like an asswhipping. I knew with my luck, I'd
get about five miles up in the woods before I slid off into a
ditch, then I'd have to walk all the way out and wake up
somebody who had a tractor while Squirrel slept it off in the
car. I wasn't just real damn happy thinking about it.

"I been ready to go home for the last three hours, and
them sorry sumbitches wouldn't even take me home," he
said.

I told him it was hell to get off with some sorry sonofabitches
who wouldn't even take you home.

"I don't mean to impo on you, Leo. You know that. Please,
please."

I didn't feel like talking. Even if I got him home without
getting stuck, it would be too late to turn around and go back
to town. And there wasn't even anything *in* town. There was
no sense in going up there looking for it. The people who
were in the bars were just as lost as I was.

"If you just get me to Aaron's. You know Aaron, don't
you?"

Well, I knew Aaron. I didn't know what Mr. Aaron would
think about me dumping Squirrel on him.

"Yeah, I know Aaron. I imagine he's in the bed asleep by
now."

"You just get me to Aaron's and I'll be all right. I wouldn't
think of impoin on you, please, please."

I told him not to sweat it, that I'd been off with drunks who
didn't want to go home, that he was in good hands now. He
talked some more about losing his eighty dollars. He said it

made him sick. A dollar was so hard to come by, he said. I clamped my lip shut and drove.

"I was on the front lines at Korea," he said. I looked sideways at him.

"I didn't know that," I said.

"Hell yes."

I listened then, because moments like that are rare, when you get to hear about these things that have shattered men's lives. I knew my daddy never got the war out of his head. When he got to drinking that's what he'd talk about. Mama said when they first got married he'd wake himself up screaming from a nightmare of hand-to-hand combat, knives and bayonets and gun stocks. With sweat all over him like he'd just stepped from water. I listened to Squirrel.

"First night out, they was fifty of our boys got killed. Just cut em all to pieces with machine guns. Half of em my friends. I mean friends like you and me. They wadn't nothing nobody could do. I can't forget about it. I thought about it all my life. Please, please."

There wasn't much I could do but listen.

"They was this one boy with me in a foxhole one night. He was my old buddy. Been knowing him ever since basic training, Fort Campbell, Kentucky. But then he got away from me and a machine gun cut loose up on top of a hill. He was screaming for me, Help me, Help me, all night long. Them goddamn bullets like to cut him half in two. Wasn't nothing I could do. You know that. I thought about it all my life. Please, please. Next morning he was dead."

There wasn't anything I could say.

"I come back off the front lines for the first time in three

months. I walked in a tent there and saw this captain standing there. I had a fifth of whiskey in my hand, and he asked
me what I wanted. I told him I wasn't looking for nothing but
a smile and a kind word. Sumbitch just cussed me and told
me to get the hell out. I laid down and cried all night long.
I've cried many a night all night long, Leo. Just get me to
Aaron's and I'll be all right."

And Daddy had seen the same things, had marched all the
way across Europe, freezing, getting shot at every day, seeing
all those people he knew die. Fighting the Germans hand to
hand. And waking up yelling, thinking he was back in it with
them again. Bayonets and knives.

"Just get me to Aaron's and I'll be all right. Please. I don't
want to impo on you. I ain't got no money to pay you, but I'll
have some later. I can go home and in five minutes I can have
a hunnerd dollars. A hunnerd dollars to me don't mean what
it used to. You boys just don't know."

"You don't want me to take you home?"

"Naw. Just take me to Aaron's. I'll get one of his cars and go
home."

"You don't think he'll get pissed off?"

"Naw. He won't get pissed off. Aaron don't care."

We pulled into Mr. Aaron's place and I parked in his yard.
Squirrel looked at me before he opened the door.

"I got to see if Aaron will let me in. You won't leave me,
will you?"

"Naw, Squirrel," I said. "I ain't gonna leave you. I'll take
you home if Aaron won't let you have a car. I'm gonna get out
and take a piss, though. I'll be right here."

I got out and stood in the rain while Squirrel staggered up to Mr. Aaron's window and knocked on the glass. I could hear him talking.

"Aaron? Aaron. Squirrel. Can I come in? Squirrel. Can I come in?"

Standing there watching him in the rain, I felt bad. He was old and withered and drunk and all he wanted was to get home so he could go to work the next day. Forget all this. Try to forget all this. But he wouldn't. He'd be back up there within a few nights. And I probably would be, too.

The light came on finally, and I saw Mr. Aaron coming to the front, his hair puffed up like wings on each side of his head. The rain fell on me. He didn't have his glasses on and he looked confused. I hollered and told Squirrel that he was coming to the front. He walked through a mud puddle and Aaron opened the door. I stepped up there and said, "I'll take him home if you don't want to mess with him, Mr. Aaron."

Squirrel stepped up beside me. "Can I come in, Aaron?" he said. "I'm trying to get home."

"Hell yeah, you can come on in," Mr. Aaron told him. He looked different without his glasses and with sleep in his eyes. He was still confused. He didn't know what was going on yet. When I was a child he treated me with kindness always. He wouldn't talk to you if he didn't know you, but he told me a lot of war stories. Squirrel walked across the boards laid on the ground that were all the porch Mr. Aaron had and stuck his hand out. We shook.

"Thanks, Leo," he said. "I'll be all right now."

They went on inside, already talking, already forgetting

about me, and I watched them for a moment before I ducked out of the rain and back into my car. I thought about things while I drove home alone. I thought about being old, and alone, and drunk and needing help. I knew I might be like that one day. I thought about having to turn to somebody for help. I hoped it would be there.

We buried Aaron today. We stood up in the church and smelled the flowers, and sang those beautiful songs over him, and the preacher said his words. I helped carry the coffin; I was one of the chosen six. It turned out that he had picked out his resting place thirty years ago. It's on high ground, in the shade, and from there you can stand and see the green hills folding away, all the way to the horizon.

I'm drinking beer now and a little into my cups, thinking about Aaron, and Squirrel, and Daddy, and about all the conversations they probably had about war. I know now that they suffered like all soldiers do, and I know they saw things that affected them for the rest of their lives.

And I just realized something. Squirrel didn't want to go home that night. He had no intention of going home. He wanted to be with somebody who knew him. And if there was anybody that night who knew what he was feeling, and what it meant, Aaron did. Aaron did for sure.

So long, old buddy. God bless you and keep you. Me, I need some sleep myself.

Sleep

My wife hears the noises and she wakes me in the night. The dream I've been having is not a good one. There is a huge black cow with long white horns chasing me, its breath right on my neck. I don't know what it means, but I'm frightened when I awake. Her hand is gripping my arm. She is holding her breath, almost.

Sometimes I sleep well and sometimes I don't. My wife hardly ever sleeps at all. Oh, she takes little naps in the daytime, but you can stand back and watch her, and you'll see what she goes through. She moans, and twists, and shakes her head no no no.

Long ago we'd go on picnics, take Sunday drives in the car. Long before that, we parked in cars and moved our hands over each other. Now all we do is try to sleep, seems like.

It's dark in the room, but I can see a little. I move my arm and my elbow makes a tiny pop. I'm thinking coffee, orange juice, two over easy. But I'm a long way away from that. And then I know she's hearing the noises once more.

"They're down there again," she says.

I don't even nod my head. I don't want to get up. It's useless anyway, and I just do it for her, and I never get through doing it. I'm warm under the covers, and the world apart from the two of us under here is cold. I think maybe if I pretend to be asleep, she'll give it up. So I lie quietly for a few moments, breathing in and out. I gave us a new electric blanket for our anniversary. The thermostat clicks on and off, with a small reassuring sound, keeping us warm. I think about hash browns, and toast, and shit on a shingle. I think about cold places I've been in. It's wonderful to do that, and then feel the warm spaces between my toes.

"Get up," she says.

Once I was trapped in a blizzard in Kansas. I was traveling, and a snowstorm came through, and the snow was so furious I drove my car right off the road into a deep ditch. I couldn't even see the highway from where I was, and I foolishly decided to stay in the car, run the heater, and wait for help. I had almost a full tank of gas. The snow started covering my vehicle. I had no overshoes, no gloves. All I had was a car coat. The windshield was like the inside of an igloo, except for a small hole where I ran the defroster. I ran out of gas after nine hours of idling. Then the cold closed in. I think about that time, and feel my nice warm pajamas.

"You getting up?" she says.

I'm playing that I'm still asleep, that I haven't heard her wake me. I'm drifting back off, scrambling eggs, warming up the leftover T-bone in the microwave, looking for the sugar bowl and the milk. The dog has the paper in his mouth.

"Did you hear me?" she says.

I hear her. She knows I hear her. I hear her every night, and it never fails to discourage me. Sometimes this getting up and down seems to go on forever. I've even considered separate beds. But so far we've just gone on like we nearly always have.

I suppose there's nothing to do but get up. But if only she knew how bad I don't want to.

"*Louis.* For God's sake. Will you get up?"

Another time I was stationed at a small base on the North Carolina coast. We had to pull guard duty at night. After a four-hour shift my feet would be blocks of ice. It would take two hours of rubbing them with my socks off, and drinking coffee, to get them back to normal. The wind came off the ocean in the winter, and it cut right through your clothes. I had that once, and now I have this. The thermostat clicks. It's doing its small, steady job, regulating the temperature of two human bodies. What a wonderful invention. I'm mixing batter and pouring it on the griddle. Bacon is sizzling in its own grease, shrinking, turning brown, bubbling all along the edges. What lovely bacon, what pretty pancakes. I'll eat and eat.

"Are you going to get up or not?"

I sigh. I think that if I was her and she was me, I wouldn't make her do this. But I don't know that for a fact. How did we know years ago we'd turn out like this? We sleep about a third of our lives and look what all we miss. But sometimes the things we see in our sleep are more horrible and magical than anything we can imagine. People come after you and try to kill you, cars go backward down the highway at seventy miles an hour with you inside and you're standing up on the brake. Sometimes you even get a little.

I lie still in the darkness and, without looking around, can see the mound of covers next to me with a gray lump of hair sticking out. She is still, too. I think maybe she's forgotten about the things downstairs. I think maybe if I just keep quiet she'll drift back off to sleep. I try that for a while. The gas heater is throwing the shadow of its grille onto the ceiling and it's leaping around. Through the black window I can see the cold stars in the sky. People are probably getting up some-where, putting on their housecoats, yawning in their fists, plugging in their Mr. Coffees.

Once I was in the army with a boy from Montana and he got me to go home with him. His parents had a large ranch in the mountains, and they took me in like another son. I'd never seen country like that Big Sky country. Everywhere you looked, all you could see was sky and mountains, and in the winter it snowed. We fed his father's cows out of a truck, throwing hay out in the snow, and boy those cows were glad to get it. They'd come running up as soon as they heard the truck. But I felt sorry for them, having to live outside in the snow and all, like deer. Once in a while we'd find a little calf that had frozen to death, frozen actually to the ground. I would be sad when that happened, thinking about it not ever get-ting to see the springtime.

I lie still under the covers in my warm bed and wonder what ever became of that boy.

Then she begins. It's always soft, and she never raises her voice. But she's dogcussing me, really putting some venom into it, the same old awful words over and over, until it hurts my ears to hear them. I know she won't stop until I get up, but I hate to feel that cold floor on my feet. She's moved my house shoes again, and I don't want to crawl under the bed looking for them. Spiders are under there, and balls of dust, and maybe even traps set for mice. I don't ever look under there, because I don't want to see what I might.

I tell myself that it's just like diving into cold water. I'll only feel the shock for a second, and that the way to do it is all at once. So I throw the covers back and I stand up. She stops talking to me. I find the flashlight on the stand beside the bed, where I leave it every night. Who needs a broken leg going down the stairs?

It's cold in the hall. I shine the flashlight on the rug, and on my gun cabinet, and for a moment I think I'll go and make coffee in the kitchen, and sit there listening to it brew, and drink a cup of it and smoke a few cigarettes. But it seems an odd time of the night to do a thing like that. The thought passes, and I go down the stairs.

I open the door to the kitchen. Of course there's nothing in there. I shut the door hard so she can hear it. I cross the dining room, lighting my way, looking at her china in the cabinet, at the white tablecloth on the table and the dust on it, and I open the door to the living room. There's nothing in there but furniture, the fireplace, some candy in a dish. I slam the door so she can hear that, too. I'm thinking of all the dreams I could be having right now, uninterrupted. It's too late for Carson, too late for Letterman, too late for Arsenio. They've all gone to bed by now.

I stand downstairs and listen to my house. I cut the light off to hear better. The silence has a noise of its own that it makes. I move to the window and push the curtains aside, but nobody's out there on the streets. It's cold out there. I'm glad I'm in here, and not out there. Still.

I sit in a chair for a little while, tapping the flashlight gently on my knee. I find my cigarettes in the pocket of my robe, and I smoke one. I don't want it, it's just a habit. It kills three or four minutes. And after that, it's been long enough. I find an ashtray with my flashlight, and put out the cigarette. I'm still thinking about that coffee. I even look in the direction of the kitchen. But finally I go ahead and climb the stairs.

I put my hand over the bulb of the flashlight when I get near the bed. I move in my own little circle of light with quiet feet. I keep my hand over it when I move it near her face. I don't want to wake her up if she's asleep. My hand looks red in the light, and my skin looks thin. I don't know how we got so old.

Her eyes are closed. She has her hands folded together, palms flat, like a child with her head resting on them. I don't know what to do with her any more. Maybe tomorrow night she won't hear the things downstairs. Maybe tomorrow night they'll be up in the attic. It's hard to tell.

I turn the flashlight off and set it back on the table beside the bed. I might need it again before the night's over. I don't want to be up stumbling around in the dark.

"Mama had three kittens," she says, and I listen. Her voice is soft, remarkably clear, like a person reciting a poem. I wait for the rest of it, but it never comes. I'm lucky, this time, I guess.

I sit on the side of the bed. I don't want to get under the covers just yet. I want to hear the house quiet again, and the silence is so loud that it's almost overpowering. Finally I lie down and pull the covers up over my head. The warmth is still there. I move toward her, looking for I don't know what. I think of a trip I took to Alaska a long time ago, when I was a young man. There were sled dogs, and plenty of snow, and polar bears fishing among cakes of ice for seals. I wonder how they can live in that cold water. But I figure it's just what you get used to. I close my eyes, and I wait.

Discipline

Please tell the court again, Mr. Lawrence.

We were tortured in pairs, singly, that is, individually, but only on Saturdays, or in groups of not more than four.

Let me see if I have this straight. Now, you said you were only tortured on Saturdays, is that right?

No. You misunderstood me. What I said was that we were only tortured individually on Saturdays.

And why do you suppose that was?

I have no idea.

[*Turns, facing the room, head shaking in mock wonderment, small malicious smile of feigned chagrin or imagined bond of friendship obvious*] You have no idea. I see. Well then, let me ask you something else. [*Referring to notes*] You said that on the evening of March twelfth, yourself and a man named Varrick? I believe? were taken from your quarters and allowed intercourse, blindfolded, with two obese women?

Well, that's partly correct. . . .

And where do you suppose—no wait. *Who* do you suppose these two women were?

I told you we were blindfolded.

Ah, yes.

And we weren't al*lowed*. We were forced. That's all in my deposition. I don't see any need to—

Just answer yes or no, please. How well did you know this Mr. Varrick? Was he a close friend?

Well. [*Perhaps hedging here?*] No. I wouldn't say he was a close friend, no. I mean we ate lunch together a few times. We read a few of each other's stories.

And you took a few showers together, too, didn't you? Yes. Did you at any time of your last period of incarceration engage in a sexual act with Mr. Varrick?

I did not.

You're under oath here, sir. Need I remind you?

Never.

Did you ever catch Mr. Varrick watching you in the shower? While you were in there together? Naked?

I never noticed.

Never noticed. I'm constantly amazed at how much you didn't notice over a period of—what was it? Five?

Four. Four years.

Four years, five years, whatever. All right. Now back to Mr. Varrick. How long did you know him?

Let's see. Let me think. I think it was . . . four, no, three years. Yes, three years. [*Nodding vigorously, hands clasped in lap*]

I think we've already established your capacity for not noticing things, but during the time you knew Mr. Varrick, did you ever happen to notice what his first name was?

I believe it was Howard.

You be*lieve* it was Howard.

Yes.

Under the contention of cruel and unusual punishment, the defense would like for us to believe that this alleged torture actually took place without due cause. Without being deserved, in other words. All right, Mr. Lawrence. Doyle Huey, isn't it? [*Titters from crowd; judge's gavel rapped lightly, perfunctorily*] You have already stated, under oath, that you and Mr. Varrick had sex with these two unidentified women.

117

I would like for you to explain to the jury and to this court exactly how you knew this act was being consummated while you were blindfolded and, apparently, engaged simultaneously in the same alleged action.

What do you mean? I don't know what you mean.

Forgive me. Let me make it simple enough for you to understand it. I mean, how did you know Mr. Varrick made love to this woman while you were blindfolded? I believe in your deposition you also stated that you were equipped with earplugs? And nose plugs? Is that correct?

That's correct. We . . . we had to breathe through our mouths. So there was no kissing. Involuntary sex, well, for involuntary sex that's required. It was just one of the rules.

And you always followed the rules.

Always tried to, yes. I mean, we were at the mercy of these people. Every time we tried to—

Let's not go off on that particular tangent again, please. Please. Just. Answer the question. How do you know Mr. Varrick had sex with this woman?

Well. I could just tell.

You could just tell. That's interesting. A prisoner for four years doesn't know why he was individually tortured only on Saturdays, doesn't know a close friend was a homosexual—

That hasn't been proved.

—isn't sure what that friend's first name was; in short, doesn't notice a whole lot about what is going on immediately around him for four years. Not very good recommendations for a writer, are they? Right?

[*Silence*]

I said, Isn't that RIGHT!

Yes. Yes. That's right.

Yet you knew without the shadow of a doubt what was going on in a cot twenty feet away, *clear across the room*, while you were blindfolded and literally deprived of any other sensory perception. Is that what you're saying?

Yes.

You're a liar. Aren't you?

No.

You *are* a liar. You've been a liar all your life, haven't you?

No.

Isn't it true that you were classified as a pathological liar by the United States Navy as early as 1966? Didn't you lie about your age to get into the Writers' Institute? Didn't you lie about the mileage on a 1963 Chevrolet Impala that you traded in Shreveport, Louisiana, for a Dodge Dart?

I . . . I don't—

Remember? Let me refresh your memory. Didn't you also take a Delco twelve-volt battery in good condition from that same Impala and replace it with a battery that actually had two dead cells, that you had been using with a trolling motor for three years?

Yes. [*With head hung*]

All *right*. Now we're getting somewhere. [*Speaking to jury*] Look at him, ladies and gentlemen! How'd you like to curl up on Christmas Eve with a good novel by him? [*Taking twenty seconds to stroll back to desk, pour glass of water, sip, reflect, study notes carefully, walk back to front*] Mr. Lawrence. Let's go back to the day you and Mr. Varrick were taken from your quarters. Why don't you just tell us about it?

Which part? You mean when we went over there? I mean, which part do you want to know about?

Why were you and Mr. Varrick selected for this alleged 'involuntary sex'? Was it because of something you had done?

I'm not sure. They never told us.

Was anybody else ever forced to perform involuntary sex with obese women? Did they just pick people out at random? Did they walk down the line and say, "Well, let's get him today"?

I don't know. We were kept isolated.

How did you and Mr. Varrick manage to read each other's stories and eat lunch a few times if you were isolated? How did you and Mr. Varrick manage to take showers together?

120

We had visitation. Everybody did.

Well, which was it?

Which was what?

Was it isolation or was it visitation? Why do you keep changing your story?

I'm not changing my story! I'm trying to tell the truth!

I don't think you are. I think you're lying. I think you've been lying since the first day of this hearing. You'd do anything to get paroled. Wouldn't you?

No.

Yes you would. You'd perjure yourself to save your own neck, wouldn't you?

I'm telling you the truth!

I don't think so.

You weren't there! You didn't have to live through it! You don't know what they made us do! [*Rising from chair halfway, hands gripping armrests*]

Control yourself, Mr. Lawrence. Just tell us. Go on.

[*Easing back. A little flustered, confused. Slight licking of lips*] Well. I guess it was about—about four o'clock in the afternoon. I was working on some revisions in my study. I remember it was almost time for beer call and I was trying to get through my revisions.

What kind of revisions are we discussing here?

Several different kinds. Some poetry. And I think, ah. Some short stories. Yes. I believe that's what it was. Well anyway. It was fifteen till four or something, and I was trying to hurry up and get through so I could turn in my revisions. We had so many each week we had to turn in for grading. But they turned on the siren ten minutes early. So, I just scooped everything up, boxed it up, then locked my study and went out to the yard.

Was Mr. Varrick in the yard when you got there?

Yes, he was.

Did you know the reason Mr. Varrick was in the camp?

Yes. [*Uneasy look. Shifting around in chair. Unable to find a comfortable position*] I did.

Would you like to tell us why Mr. Varrick was in the camp?

[*Extremely uneasy. Rubbing palms together, averting his face, appearing to be searching for something at his feet*] Well. It was common knowledge, I suppose. He was in for plagiarism. Like seventy-five percent of the other inmates.

Was this a first offense for Mr. Varrick?

I'm . . . I'm not sure. [*Obviously lying*]

Right. Not sure. Can't remember. Didn't notice. Isn't it true that Mr. Varrick had in fact had his probation revoked for plagiarism?

Well . . . yes. But it wasn't the same author.

Oh? Your memory seems to be improving. I don't suppose you'd remember who he plagiarized the first time, would you?

I believe it was Flannery O'Connor. I think it was a line out of "A Good Man Is Hard to Find."

A line? Is that right? One line?

I believe so. Yes. I'm sure that's what it was.

[*Shaking his head. Wry humor touched with pity*] Mr. Lawrence. Didn't Mr. Varrick actually copy, ver*b*atim, every single word from the time the grandmother's family went into The Tower, until they had the wreck? And turn it into *Playboy* as his own?

[*Shaken badly now*] I don't know. I—didn't know it was that bad.

Bad? You don't think it's bad to steal from a dead woman? Pilfer words from a sick, dying writer, who barely had the strength to work three hours a day? Who had more guts and talent in one little finger than you and your buddy Varrick have in your whole bodies?

I didn't mean that! I meant I didn't know he stole that much!

Stole! That's the right word. Robbed. [*With vigor*] Extorted. That's a better word. But even that. Even *that* wasn't as bad as what he did later. Was it? It wasn't as bad as what got him thrown in hacks' prison for five years, was it?

No. [*Almost whispering*] It wasn't.

Well. You're telling it. Your memory's coming back now, isn't it? Why don't you just tell us what he did do? After he was already on probation for the same crime?

I told you. It was plagiarism. Why do I have to say all this? You know it already. You know what he did!

Didn't it ever strike you that Mr. Varrick might have been just a little bit stupid?

Well. I suppose so.

You suppose so? Is that all you can say? You suppose so?

All right. It was stupid.

Who did he plagiarize the next time, Mr. Lawrence? The five-year sentence. And please don't tell me what you believe.

[*Grim, fatalistic conviction of lethargic hopelessness*] It was Cormac McCarthy.

Well, well. Now we're getting somewhere again. Now we're talking about *living* writers. Now we're getting up to a new level of theft. We're getting up into grant country now. Now we're talking about the American Academy of Arts and Letters. The big time.

Yes. [*Whispered*]

You're telling it so good I think I'll just let you go on. Why don't you just tell us what Mr. Varrick did to Mr. McCarthy?

[*Studying fingernails*] He stole different passages from three of his novels.

And?

And submitted—

Wait, wait. First—

First he put them into his own novel.

It was actually a novella, wasn't it?

I don't know. I never read it.

You never read it because it was never published. It was never published because it was submitted to the same house that originally published those same three novels. Ladies and gentlemen, the act of a stupid man. He stole ten thousand words, whole, uncut scenes, dialogue, ripped them up a little, tore them up some, and mixed them with ten thousand of his own miserable words and called it his own. Didn't he?

Yes. Yes, he did.

And he got caught.

Yes.

Just like you got caught.

Yes.

In a blatant, vicious act of plagiarism. Literary theft. And it got him five years.

Yes.

Did Mr. Varrick ever confide in you? Did he ever tell you any of his secrets?

Secrets? [*Shrugs shoulders, still studying nails*] We talked. Some.

Did he ever say to you that he thought his sentence was unfair?

[*Looking up*] Yes. He did.

What exactly did he say?

He said . . . he said he thought it was too long. And he said he thought the regimen was too strict. He said he thought we should have more beer and more recreational reading. More contemporary reading.

Like what?

Oh, you know. More new stuff. He thought we should have been allowed to read what was on the best-seller lists.

In short, he didn't want to have to read the classics, correct? He just wanted to skip Melville and Twain and Tolstoy, didn't he?

Essentially, yes. That's correct.

He thought they were a bunch of old geezers, didn't he?

Well. Not in so many words. I guess you could put it like that.

Didn't he actually say that once, though? Didn't he once, in the presence of two other prisoners, call Sophocles 'a dried-up old fart'?

I . . .

You don't remember.

No.

Your memory just comes and goes, doesn't it? Well, why don't you just see if you can remember what happened on the afternoon you met Mr. Varrick in the yard, before you were taken in for involuntary sex? I'm sure everybody would just love to hear that.

It may take a while.

I've got all day.

[*Deep breath, gathering will*] Well. Like I said, we thought it was beer call. I mean, it was almost four o'clock. We just thought they were a little early.

Were they ever early for a beer call?

Not usually, no.

Up until that time, had you ever seen an early beer call?

No.

Wasn't everything timed to a very strict schedule, right up to the minute?

Yes. Well anyway. I saw How—Mr. Varrick, standing in line on the yellow footprints, and I went over to him. We talked for a minute. He'd been writing some poetry—

Whose? Raymond Carver's?

and he said he thought something funny was going on. He said they'd been heavy on his grading. He said all his papers were coming back with red marks on them, and they'd caught him with three comma splices in one week. And he'd lost his thesaurus. He was worried.

Under oath, Mr. Lawrence. Did he mention anything to you at that time about involuntary sex?

He said . . . he said he thought we were in for it. Those were his words.

He didn't specifically mention involuntary sex?

No. Not in so many words. I just told you what he said.

But you knew. You knew what was coming.

We didn't know for sure. They hadn't told us anything.

You knew it wasn't beer call yet. Didn't you?

Well, everybody else was beginning to line up. They all had their papers. We hadn't been given any reason to suspect. We . . . we thought they'd let us slide. At least, I did.

And why was that? Had they ever let anybody slide before?

[*Ghastly smile, horrific remembrance, flood of emotions rapidly flickering across face*] No. They never had.

Then why did you think this time would be any different? Why did you think they weren't going to take you out and torture you? Were you friendly with any of the guards?

No. Certainly not. They were all former editors. That was one of the requirements.

I'm well aware of the requirements. This court is not questioning the integrity of the guards.

It should! If you call yourselves lawmakers! This hearing is a farce! Howard Varrick was a humorist! If he'd been published he'd have been one of the greatest writers of this century! He was on his way! He was making some real progress until he was tortured! I read his drafts! I laughed!

[*General confusion, buzzing from peanut gallery, rapping of gavel, uneasy order quickly restored. Small gaping faces at door swiftly pushed outside*] Thank you. [*Turning, pausing, acknowledging appreciation to judge*] If we can proceed. . . . Tell us about that afternoon. Tell us what happened after you and Mr. Varrick discussed your problems.

We had to turn our papers in. That came first. Dr. Evans was the personal guard and senior editor.

Did Dr. Evans review your revisions in the exercise yard?

Yes. He did. But that was common practice. We had to get the initial okay from him before we could go to beer call.

And how long did that usually take?

[*Ruminating, chin in hand*] Not long, usually. He'd just give it a quick glance. He wouldn't read all the way through.

How long would you say? Ten minutes? Five?

Probably about five. Maybe a little less.

And how many words of copy are we talking about here?

Well. It varied.

How much?

It depended. On what we were revising.

How many words would you say, on the day in question?

Between us?

Yes, Between you.

Oh. Probably. About six thousand. Somewhere around that.

He was a fast reader, wasn't he?

Fairly quick, I suppose. I'm sure he'd had a lot of practice.

But you didn't go to beer call that day. Did you?

No. We didn't.

What did it, Mr. Lawrence?

I don't understand.

Whose work was it that caused Dr. Evans to cancel your beer break and send you in for involuntary sex instead?

[*Mad panic now, sudden, furious, eyes searching the court, hands gripping chair arms wildly*] What?

I said whose work was it?

I don't have to answer that question!

Answer it.

No.

Answer it!

Damn you! Damn you and your court. I'm not saying anything else. I want to see my lawyer.

Well, there he is. Sitting right there at that table.

[*Unable to decide. Fear. Horror. Mouth chewing knuckle*] I . . .

Answer the question. Wasn't it in fact *your* work that got Mr. Varrick sent in for involuntary sex along with you? Hadn't he been cribbing your notes? Didn't you drag him down with you? Weren't you still secretly copying Faulkner, at *night*, under the covers, with a flashlight?

Eee . . . yes! Damn you! Yes!

Weren't you laboring along, in the 'great southern gothic tradition,' using heavy, frightening imagery?

Yes! [*Beaten. Whipped. Chastised. Chastened. Cowed. Diminished. Uncertain. Afraid. Tentative. Sick*]

Ignoring punctuation, running whole pages of narrative together, incorporating colons, semicolons, hyphens, making your characters talk like Beeder Mackey on LSD?

[*Softly*] Yes.

All right. What happened after Dr. Evans finished reading your . . . *work*?

[*Trying to regain composure*] He became irrational.

Irrational? Was it irrational for him to show displeasure over unacceptable work?

No.

Was it irrational for him to have little patience with two longtime inmates who refused to be rehabilitated? Repeaters?

No.

Then why did you say he became irrational?

He . . . [*shifting in chair, crossing legs, uncrossing legs*] he started taking the paper clips off the papers. He was shouting.

What was he shouting?

Obscenities.

Were these obscenities pertaining to the work at hand?

Yes.

Did he tell you he was about to take you in for involuntary sex?

No. He didn't. He just told us to wait, that we weren't going to beer call with the rest.

What happened then?

Well. We waited. We waited in the yard.

Did everybody else take a beer break?

Yes. They did. We could hear them. They sounded like they were having a good time.

Really whooping it up, eh?

Yes.

And that really bothered you. Didn't it?

Yes. It did.

You thought you weren't being treated fairly, didn't you? You thought even a convicted copycat should have rights, didn't you?

Yes. I do. I mean I did.

When did you first realize that you were about to be taken in for involuntary sex?

When they brought the blindfolds out.

Were the earplugs and the nose plugs applied at this time, also?

Yes. They were. [*Eyes downcast*] We knew, then.

Were you afraid?

I . . . [*Ashamed*] I was very afraid. I'd never had to do anything like that before in my life.

But you'd been given plenty of warning.

Yes.

You'd been told to pick up the level of your writing. Both of you.

Yes.

Were you blindfolded before you were taken inside?

No, they—made us look at them first. For several minutes.

And then.

[*A whisper*] Then they blindfolded us. [*Whole court straining forward to catch words, reporters scribbling furiously*] I tried to hold Howard's hand but I couldn't find it. I told him . . . I told him to be brave. He was crying. I was, too. We were both . . . at the lowest point of our lives. They'd reduced us to animals.

What happened then?

[*Eyes closed. Huge gulp*] Someone touched me. She said —she said she was a member of a book club. And a poetry society. She put her arms around me. They were big arms. Huge.

Were you scared?

I was terrified.

Can you describe it?

Describe *what*? Do you want to hear about the *act*? Oh, you
filthy animal. You dirty, dirty man. You want to hear about it?
I'll tell you about it. I'll tell you all you want to hear. If it'll
keep one person from going through what I went through.
She was fat, okay? She was big, and fat, and heavy, and she
sweated, all right? [*Rising from chair, face heated, turning
red, carotid artery protuberant, teeth gritted*] She couldn't
have sat down in two chairs, okay? She didn't have any teeth.
She was covered with tattoos and she was hairy, and she had
bad breath. Now. You want to hear some more?

Bailiff?

No! She got on top of me! They'd told her I was famous! She
was mashing me! I was trying to get out from under her but
she was too big! It was horrible, do you hear me? Horrible! I
can't forget about it! I wake up in the night screaming from it,
screaming from it, screaming huh huh huh. . . . [*Complete
breakdown, hands over face, gradual grading off to racking
sobs loud in hushed awe of courtroom*]

All right, Mr. Lawrence. [*Going back to table for manuscript
pages, waving them in the air*] The state has one more piece
of evidence to present in this parole hearing. [*Approaching
witness stand, thrusting papers rudely forward*] Read this.
Out loud.

[*Looking up, face still contorted, eyes wet, nose snuffling*] What?

[*Shaking pages belligerently*] You wrote it. I should think you'd be proud to get a chance to read it in public. I want this court to hear the real reason your parole should be denied. Go on, read it.

[*Taking papers slowly, recognizing them*] Oh. God, no. [*Head shaking, papers trembling slightly in fingers*] You can't mean . . . I don't want to read this. Please. It isn't fair to make me read this. If you have one shred of decency . . .

Read it.

This . . . this is just a rough draft.

I thought you'd revised it, Mr. Lawrence.

I was drunk when I wrote this.

Wasn't beer call yet, Mr. Lawrence. Remember? Read it.

You. You got this out of my files somehow. This was locked up in my study. [*Looking up, amazed*] You won't stop, will you? It's never going to end, is it? You want to keep me in there forever, don't you? You don't really believe in rehabilitation. It's just a way to keep us out of print. [*Soft, unbelievable horror. Pause. Bitter resignation. Determination*] All right, I'll read it. I'll read every damn word of it. It may be the only time I'll get to. [*Bracing himself, adjusting tie, one hand on knee, beginning . . .*] And it was with a timorous expression of the wide upturned Afro-American nostrils that, arched and slightly hissing, Otis McQuay paused and turned toward his eating, sitting, brother, the twin, the Aquarius, the one with whom he had shared the dark bloody nacreous unlighted cavern of his mother's womb, and sniffed, hesitantly, not blatantly or in open astonishment or anything so challenging as that, at the malodorous gases drifting cloudlike and thick as turtle soup down the rough unplaned splintered wobbly table to where he sat eating his butter beans and cornbread, his stance like that of a bluetick on a mess of birds. For it was not in his nature to be challenging. Then he heard it, the slight thin whistle like steam escaping, and his eyes shifted quickly in their sockets, huge and white and rolling. Trapped, with him now, his own supper but half eaten, frozen in that indecision or flight or willingness to endure, to stand, the muscles of his legs coiled tight as screen-door springs, his hands on either side of his plate like dead or wounded or dying blackbirds, while all around him the fumes grew stronger and more malodorous, more pungent. The air grew rank, grew right funky. There came a long ragged sound like paper tearing and it was chopped off short, immeasurably loud in the close silence. Then like two toots on a bugle came the next two toots: toot, toot. But it was not the brass mouth of a trumpet, not an instrument of music that played that sorry scale. It was something deeper, more sinister —

I think that will do.

a sound born not of clean air and lungs but a fecund, a ripe smell, like burning shoes . . .

Your Honor, I think we've proved our point. . . . Bailiff, would you show this man to his seat?

. . . like dead rattlesnakes, like soured slops, like contaminated sheepdip—

Could we get the bailiffs to perform their duties, please?

[*Bailiffs surging forward, babble of voices rising from courtroom, judge rapping gavel*]

Like moldy mattress stuffings! Like bad cheese!

Your Honor! Could we have order restored! Please!

[*Judge rapping gavel louder, bailiffs grappling with defendant on witness stand, now wild-eyed, smiling! Defiant! Eyes ablaze!*] Like putrid prairie dog meat! Wait! There's more! Do you hear me! Just listen!

92 Days

for buk

1

Monroe came over to see me one day, shortly after I divorced. He had some beer. I was glad to see him. I was especially glad to see his beer.

"How you taking it?" he said.

"Pretty good, I guess."

"Have a beer."

"Thanks."

"Women," he said. "Jesus Christ."

"Right."

We sat there and drank his beer. I was almost out of money. I was too upset to write anything. I'd tried it a few times, and wound up just gnawing my knuckles. I was afraid I'd lost it for good. I was almost out of food, too.

"When you gonna get a job?"

"I don't know. I need one. I need some money."

"I can let you paint houses for me a few days."

"Thanks, Monroe."

I started that afternoon. It went pretty well. It was soothing, mindless work, and I didn't have to think. I thought plenty, but not about what I was doing. What I had decided to do was just live hand to mouth. Work a few days and then quit and live off the money and write until the money was gone. Then work a few more days, and so on. It was a spur-of-the-moment plan, and as soon as I planned that, I promised myself I'd never plan anything else as long as I lived.

At the end of three days Monroe gave me a hundred and eighty dollars. I bought some food and some beer. That was all I needed. Well, two cartons of Marlboros. I had a place to stay. I had a bed, a chair, some books and records.

The first night I just sat there looking at a blank sheet of paper.

Next night, same thing. Nothing would come. I knew I'd lost it. I'd have to be a house painter for the rest of my life.

The third night I typed one paragraph and threw it away. The fourth night I started a new story.

2

I got a letter back in the mail along with a manuscript of one of my novels from an agent in New York. I read the letter while I drank a beer and smoked a cigarette. It said (along with Dear Mr. Barlow):

We are returning your novel not because it is not publishable, but because the market at this time is not amenable to novels about drunk pulpwood haulers and rednecks and deer hunting. Our comments relate more to its marketability than to its publishability, and even though this novel is hilarious in many places and extremely well-written with a good plot, real characters, refreshing dialogue, beautiful descriptions and no typographical or spelling errors, we don't feel confident that we could place it for you. We would, however, be delighted to read anything else you have written or will write in the future.

It was signed by some asshole. I didn't read his name. I rolled a piece of paper into the machine and wrote my own letter. It said:

You, sir, are an ignorant man. How the fuck do you know it won't sell if you don't try to sell it? And do you think I can just shit another one on five minutes' notice? I worked on this cocksucker for two years. You got any idea what that takes out of a man? You like to play God with all of us out here, is that it? You kept my manuscript for three months and didn't even send it around. Here I was thinking the whole time that maybe somebody was thinking about buying it. I wish I had you down here. I'd whip your ass. I'd stomp a mud hole in your ass and walk it dry.

You turd head. I hope you lose your job. You're not worth a fuck at it anyway. I hope your wife gives you the clap. I wish I had your job and you had mine. How'd you like to paint a few houses while it's a hundred degrees? I can tell you it's not any fun. I hope you get run over by a taxi cab on your way home. And then die after about a month of agonizing pain.

I rolled the letter up and read it. I thought it was pretty good. It expressed my feelings exactly. It made me feel a whole lot better. I read it twice and then I took it out of the machine and tore it up and threw it away. Then I started working on my story.

At four a.m. I was still working on it. I liked working in the middle of the night. There wasn't any noise anywhere. You didn't have to think about anything but what you had right in front of you.

I finished the story, read it, then addressed an envelope and stuck a few stamps on it and put the story inside it and carried it out the door, down the driveway to the mailbox. I knew it would go off for a while and then probably come back with a marvelous note on the rejection slip.

I was knocking, had been knocking for years, but it was taking a long time for them to let me in.

I went back inside, turned off the lights, and went to bed. Alone.

3

Lots of friends came by to see me. One of them was Raoul. Raoul had been in the crop-duster business and had made a fortune by flying in a load of marijuana to Jackson, Tennessee, one night. He had cousins in Caracas. He had plenty of money, and now he was trying to write. He wrote poetry mostly, and wanted me to read it. The night he came over he had three or four poems. He also had a lot of beer with him. I was glad to see him. I wasn't so glad to see his poems.

"Hey, Barlow, I've got some new poems," he said.

He'd caught me at the typewriter, in the act itself, which, of course, was almost sacred to me.

"I'm kind of busy, Raoul. I'm trying to write."

"Oh, come on, man, I brought you some beer. Sit down and read these poems."

I hated to have to mess with him, but I was almost out of beer.

"The only way I'll read them is if you leave me some beer, Raoul. I'm trying to write."

"Hey, man, take all the beer you want. You understand this shit, Barlow. Read these poems. Tell me what you think about them."

Raoul sat on the couch and I started looking at his poems.

"I've got some women we can pick up later, Barlow."

"Great, Raoul."

The first poem was about a bullfighter. There was a lot of blood and sand in it. There was a lot of death in the afternoon. The bullfighter was a candyass, though; he couldn't face the bulls. Finally he ran from one and got a horn rammed up his ass and had to have a colectomy. And then he just stayed on a cot in a cantina for the rest of his life, sucking on a tequila bottle.

"This poem sucks, Raoul." I laid it aside and picked up the next one. "I think it'd be a lot better if you tried to make a short story out of it."

"I know, man, I know. I don't know the prose, though, man, I don't know the *prose.*"

The next poem was about a garbageman who tried to smell the roses in life every day. And as bad as it was, Raoul had his finger on something. He was touching the hurt in people, trying to. For that I gave him an A.

"Listen, Raoul, you're a good guy. You've got some humanity in you even if you did put a lot of dope on the streets of Jackson, Tennessee."

"It was just a one-time thing, man."

"Listen, Raoul, none of that shit matters. If you want to write, you've got to shut yourself up in a room and write."

"I've been thinking about doing that, man."

I got one of his beers and looked at the next poem. It was called "Viva Vanetti." It was about a Mafia hit man who weighed four hundred pounds and was nicknamed the "Salsa Sausage." He went around killing people by submerging their heads in vats of pizza dough.

"This one sucks, too, Raoul."

"Read the next one, man."

"How can you write good stuff one minute and such crappy stuff the next?"

"I don't know, man. It just comes to me."

I swore for a little bit and then picked up the last poem. It started off hot. The narrator was screaming things about lost pussy, and alleycats rutting behind garbage cans. It had the heat of a summer night in the city in it. It had people on dope, switchblades, and cops who slapped the hell out of people and screamed in their faces. It had people trapped on fire escapes and gorillas loose from the zoo. It had everything in it. I was a little pissed that I hadn't written it. It was A-OK.

"It's great, Raoul. Son of a bitch is great. It'll be published."

I didn't tell him that might take ten or fifteen years.

"No shit, man? No *shit*?"

"I don't know how you did it," I said. "You ought to try writing some stories."

Raoul got up and started walking around the room.

"Wow, man," he said. "Wow!"

"Let's go get the women, Raoul," I said. I was ready for the women.

"Oh, shit, man, we can't go get the women now! I've got to go home and type up a clean copy of that poem. I've got to get that poem in the mail, man!"

Then he rushed right out the door. Then he rushed right back in and snatched the poem out of my hands.

"Thanks a million, Barlow! I'll never forget you for this!"

I drank four or five more of his beers and thought about the unfairness of everything. A guy like Raoul could make one big score and have it dicked for the rest of his life. But poetry was a hobby for him. It wasn't life and death for him. All he wanted was to see his name in a magazine. He wouldn't starve for his art. I was down to thirty-two dollars, and about to starve for mine.

I started writing another story.

4

My *mother* came to see me. I'd had about four beers that afternoon. I knew she was going to lay a lot of stuff on me that I didn't want to hear.

"How are you doing?" she said.

"I'm doing all right."

"Have you seen the children?"

"Not lately."

"Well, what are you going to *do*?"

I wanted to reach for a beer but I'd been raised not to drink in front of my mother.

"What else? I'm going to keep writing."

"After all it's cost you."

"Right."

"After you've lost your whole family over it."

"Wouldn't make a whole lot of sense to stop now, would it?"

She started crying. I knew she would. I went ahead and got the beer. She was probably thinking How did I ever raise this cold-blooded child?

I sat down with her.

"Look, Mama, I can't help it that I want to do this. It's not even a matter of wanting to. I *have* to. I can't live without it."

"Well, how are you going to live? You don't even have a job."

I looked out the window.

"I work when I need the money. I paint a house once in a while. I work for a while and then I write for a while. I'm okay. Don't worry about me."

"It's my grandchildren I worry about. How are you going to pay your child support? When are you going to get to see them?"

"I guess I'll see them when she lets me. Have you seen them?"

"Yes."

"What did they say?"

"They wanted to know when you were coming home."

Then she started crying again.

5

I hadn't made love in about sixty-four days, which is not an easy thing after you've been married and used to getting it whenever you want it. I didn't know many women and had great difficulty communicating with them. Most of the women I did know were friends of my ex-wife or wives of my friends. I was never able to tell women just exactly what I thought about womanhood in general, what wonderful things I thought women were. I had composed several poems about women that I had not submitted to any of the literary quarterlies, but basically they sang the praises of legs and breasts and long hair and painted toenails, red lips and nipples. Once in a while I would take these poems out and read them and then put them away again.

I missed my children. They were big holes torn out of my life. I knew that I had torn a big hole out of their lives. I hoped that their mother would have the good sense to marry a good man who would take care of them and give them a home, educations, food, love. I knew there'd never be a reconciliation. Their mother didn't want it, and I didn't want it. Our children and our parents were probably the only ones who wanted it. I only had one life, and I'd be damned if I'd live it in a way that would make me unhappy and please somebody else. I had already lived that kind of life, too much of it already.

6

The money ran out and I knew I'd have to go back to work. I knew also that my ex-wife's lawyer would soon be dunning me for an alimony payment which I didn't have. I considered full-time employment for about fifteen seconds, and then realized that since I had made the choice to be sorry, I wanted to be sorry full-time.

I went back to painting houses. I painted houses in Oxford, in Taylor, in Toccopola, in Dogtown. I wore paint-spattered clothes and let my hair and beard grow out. I wrote at night, with beer in the cooler on the floor next to the desk. All of my stories came back in. I bought a small postage scale and weighed my own envelopes to the penny and mailed them back out. Nothing, nothing. Nobody wanted my work. Sometimes I wrote all night and staggered out the door the next morning to paint houses. I painted houses for twenty-three days straight and then took the money and retired again. I hit the grocery store first. Forty pounds of leg quarters that I could fry and keep cold in the fridge. Salami and baloney. Cheese. Chili and hot dogs. I got a few brown steaks that were already frozen, perfectly good cheap meat. The rest of the cart I filled up with beer and cigarettes.

They were good days. I slept late and got up and read the newspaper and made coffee and breakfast, then sat down and started writing. Stories, nothing but stories. The last novel had taken me two years, and I wasn't ready to commit to that kind of time again right away. I could write a story in two days, revise it in a couple of hours, and be ready to start another one. I wrote through the afternoons, stopped for a while to fix something for supper, then went back to writing again. There was nothing I could do but keep going. I had already made all my decisions.

7

I thought she looked bad when I saw her. She was coming into a bar with some other people just as I was going out. She saw me and she stopped, so I had to stop, too. The people with her spoke briefly, friends of ours, friends of hers, ex-friends of mine, evidently. People who had been to our house and eaten with us and shared our wine and music. Or maybe they just wanted to get out of the way. I didn't blame them. The end hadn't been nice. The end had been nasty. Nasty people and nasty words and phrases and nastiness to make you go puke in the gutter. Me, her: both of us.

I didn't ask where the kids were. I didn't want to seem accusatory. I didn't want to seem drunk, but I was. I'd been in there for four hours. I was on my way to try and weave my key into the ignition. Everything that might be said would be forgotten the next morning. Just a black hole with her somewhere standing in it, a picture of her face to rock to sleep against your pillow.

"Hey," she said.

"Hey."

"You leaving?"

"Me? Well, yeah, I think so. What you up to?"

"Oh, nothing. Just out here looking for somebody to fuck. Right?"

"I don't know."

"Well, I am. Fucking everybody I can. You know how that goes, trying to fuck everybody you can."

I didn't say anything, so she went on by herself.

"Yeah, I'm trying to get enough together to have a gangbang about midnight if I can. If I can find enough of them still sober enough to fuck. A lot of men have that problem, you know. Start drinking beer about nine o'clock in the morning and drink all day and then have a bad case of the limpdick about dark."

"You doing okay?" I said.

"Nah. Ain't getting enough dick. This one of your hangouts, huh?"

"I come here sometimes."

"I bet there's some real sluts in here. It must be."

"You seem to be in here."

"Yeah, I just got here, though."

"Where's the kids?"

"None of your fucking business. Where's my money?"

"What money?"

"Oh. You ain't got my letter from my lawyer yet?"

"No."

"You'll get it tomorrow, probably. He mailed it yesterday. I hope you're ready to fork over your alimony payment of three hundred and twenty-five dollars."

"Three twenty-five? I thought it was one seventy-five."

"You get to pay the lawyer fees. He don't like waiting on his money. You're paying him a hundred and fifty for five months. Then you can go back to one seventy-five but after that I'm going to ask the judge to raise it back to three twenty-five since I ain't getting enough with two kids to feed and a house payment to make. You fucked anybody in here tonight?"

I just looked at her for a minute.

"Why does there have to be all this ugliness? Why do you have to act like this? Do you hate me that bad?"

"You goddamn right I do. And I'm gonna make you pay for every night I have to stay by myself."

"I don't have that kind of money."

"You better shit it then. Your mama said you'd been painting houses."

"Well. Some."

"Well, the kids ain't asked about you. I told them you left us. You better paint plenty of houses is all I can say."

"I'm not working that much. I'm trying to write, too."

"Ha! You better forget that shit. You're not gonna divorce

me and then think you're gonna get to do what you want to. Uh uh, honey. Me and these kids come first. You brought em into this world and you're gonna take care of em till they're twenty-one. And if that don't leave you enough time for your life, tough shit."

"Why do you have to make me so mad? Why do you have to make me want to bust your face open for you?"

"I just wish you'd try it. I'd have your ass stuck in that jail so fast it'd make your head swim."

"When do I get the kids?"

"When I get ready."

"That's not what the judge said."

"Well, you just let me know when you want em. They can be sick sometimes, you know. They *can* be out of town."

All she wanted was for me to fall on my knees and grab her leg and beg to be taken back, so she'd have the enjoyment of turning me down. All she wanted was to be filled with hatred and bitterness for the rest of her life, and to turn her life into a secret and twisted and perverted thing that would torment her as badly as it would me. You read about these killings in the paper, between men and women, husbands and wives, ex-Adams and Eves? This is how they happen.

8

If I killed anybody that night, I didn't know anything about it the next morning. I woke hot, sweating, dizzy with the heat. I pulled down all the windows and blinds, turned on the air conditioner, and made some coffee. While it was perking I picked up a clock and looked at it. 11:30. The mail had already run, surely. I put on a pair of blue jeans and slipped my feet into my house shoes and went down the driveway. There were three manila envelopes inside the mailbox. I went back to the house with the little mothers tucked under my arm.

I poured myself a cup of coffee and stirred some sugar into it, didn't have any milk. I lit my first cigarette. I was almost out of beer again, but I hoped Monroe would leave me alone.

The news was bad, but it was news I was used to. I sat down on the couch with my coffee and my cigarettes and an ashtray and the three stories. All I could remember was her being nasty to me, and something about a pine tree being hung under my wheel on the way home. I looked at my tennis shoes on the floor. They had mud and pine needles on them. I opened the first envelope.

It was a plain rejection slip from *Spanish Fly*. On it was scrawled: *Nice, try again*. And some scribbled initials. What? Nice but not nice enough to publish? Nice enough to publish but you've got two years' worth of stories already accepted? Explain yourself here. Somebody might be getting ready to hang himself over this shit. What about Breece D'J Pancake? What about John Kennedy Toole? *Nice, try again* might have driven them over the edge.

I was silently weeping. I had anger. I tore open the second envelope. I knew it would be more of the same. There was a long, neatly typed letter from the assistant editor of *Ivory Towers* that said (along with Dear Leon):

This story came so close to being accepted. Majority rules and many people who read it misinterpreted it. We have had an argument for two weeks here over it. "White Girls with Black Asses," do you think you could tone that down a little bit, maybe change it to something else? Because the story doesn't really fit the title. And although it works wonderfully, what is the reason that Cleve beats his wife? He is always remorseful after he does it, enough to where he lashes himself to the tree in the lightning storm. Some people were revulsed by it. I must say it's one of the strongest things I've seen in a while. I would never tell you how to write. But maybe if you changed the title another magazine might be interested in it. We would love to see anything else you would care to send us. Please keep writing. Don't let this be disappointing to you. You have great talent, and with material like this you will need great stamina.

All warmest wishes,
Betti DeLoreo

The next question was, what did Betti DeLoreo, Betti Del Oreo, look like? Was she married? Was she seventy years old? Would she be willing to meet with me and give me some of her nooky on the strength of my work? They were uncertain questions, and my hands were shaking just to think that a letter might come back one day minus the story I'd sent off.

I opened the third envelope. It contained a story that had been going around for two years. There was a rejection slip from *Blue Lace* attached to it. It seemed that my material was not right for them; however, it was no reflection on the work itself, and they were sorry they were unable to make individual comments on each story because of their small staff, et cetera.

9

I went to town to get some more beer. I hadn't been answering my phone, even though it had rung several times. I knew it might be the lawyer, and I knew it might be Monroe, wanting me to go back to work. I had enough money to tide me over for a little while, and I didn't want to go back to painting houses until I had to. I knew the alimony payment would have to be reckoned with before long, and that was making me nervous, and I needed something to drink while I worked. It seemed like the harder I tried, the worse things became. I wondered how other people dealt with it. I tried to bury myself in my work, forget my feelings and my shortcomings and my fears and the sick weak hangovers that accompanied a night of writing and drinking. In winter it would be too cold to paint houses and what would I do then for money? I could work for the rest of the summer and try to save a little, but there wouldn't be any way I could save enough to pay the alimony. If I couldn't pay it, she'd have me put in jail. But maybe I'd be able to write in jail. I hoped I would.

I went into a grocery store to get the beer. Usually I went to wherever it was the cheapest. I got beer, barbecued pigskins, Slim Jims to munch on while writing. Sometimes when the muse wouldn't hit I had to have something to do and sometimes chewing worked. I had to have a cart to hold every-thing. When I got to the checkout I had to wait in line. I saw people looking at the things in my basket. I ignored them and looked instead at the covers of *Cosmopolitan* and *The National Enquirer.* Religious freaks had made them hide the *Playboy*s and *Penthouse*s under the counters several years before. The whole world seemed to be trying to be decent, and I seemed an indecent thing in it. I wanted titties, lots of them. I wanted to hear ZZ Top play "Legs." I wanted to live in a house on a hill with a swimming pool and a cool back porch where my friends could listen to music after I mixed them drinks. I looked at what I wanted and then I looked at what I had. There was a great gulf between the two of them. My clothes were stained with paint, and my fingernails were dirty. I wanted my children somehow without their mother. The woman rang up my purchases and they came to $29.42, including tax.

10

I knew I hadn't exhausted the possibilities in New York, but they had nearly exhausted me. I knew that publishers were men and women like men and women here, that they breathed, ate, read, got bored, watched TV. My novel had been to so many offices it had become dog-eared, but I didn't want to retype it. That would have been about a two-week job, possibly for nothing.

I sat there looking at it. It was just a stack of typed paper an inch and a half thick. But I knew there was nothing wrong with it. I knew that all it would take would be for the right person to see it. So far that hadn't happened.

I opened my copy of *Writer's Market* to the section that lists commercial publishers and closed my eyes. I flipped pages this way and that, flipped some more, flipped some backwards, then forward again. I stabbed a page with my finger, and then opened my eyes. I located a name, an address, and copied them onto a large manila envelope. I mailed it without hope or dread, without a covering letter, without retyping it. I just mailed it.

11

The letter from the lawyer came in the mail. It said (along with Dear Mr. Leon Barlow):

My fees for handling your divorce trial and proceedings amount to $750.00. I would like to be paid as soon as possible, of course, but Mrs. Barlow has informed me that you are in a state of near penury. Therefore we have worked out a schedule of payments by figuring $150/ month along with your alimony payment. This will be deducted by me before turning over the remainder to Mrs. Barlow each month. Your first payment is due immediately and four more payments thereafter on the 1st of each month. Please remit your payment by return mail.

It was signed by that lawyer, I didn't read his name. I had forty-seven dollars to my name. I wondered if the jail still fed only twice a day. The only time I had been a weekend guest of that establishment, they had.

12

My uncle came by to see me. He was the brother of my mother, the only one who seemed to understand what I was trying to do. He had no love of reading or even movies except westerns, but he admired will and determination in a person no matter the odds, and he liked to see a man try to rise above his station in life.

"What are you doing?" he said.

"Nothing. Drinking a beer. You want one?"

"I might drink one. You're not writing anything?"

"Yessir, I'm writing. I'm writing every day. I'm just not publishing anything."

"Why not?"

"I don't know."

"Is it good enough to publish?"

"Yes. It is."

"How do you know?"

"Because I read the other stuff they publish."

"You think it's politics?"

"I don't know what it is."

"How you fixed for money?"

"Pretty bad. I've got to get out and find some work."

"You want me to give you a cow? I can give you a couple of cows if it would help you."

"What good's a couple of cows gonna do me?"

"Hell, dumb butt. Carry em to the sale and sell em. They're worth five or six hundred apiece."

"I hate to take anything from you. Marilyn's trying to wring my balls dry with alimony, though."

"I know it. She'll do it, too. Any time a man gets divorced in Missippi he's gonna pay through the nose. She letting you see the kids?"

"No. I haven't seen them a time."

"Take her back to court."

"I'd owe a lawyer some more money then."

"She's fucking over you, though. You just gonna lay here and take it?"

"I don't seem to have much choice."

My uncle got up and snorted. "There's always a choice." He drained his beer and tossed the can into the trash. "Come over to the house tomorrow and we'll catch those cows, load em up, haul em to the sale. They ought to bring eleven or twelve hundred anyway."

"What time?"

"Early. We need to be at New Albany by two."

"I'll be there. Thanks, Uncle Lou."

"Don't mention it."

13

My uncle had so many cows he didn't know exactly how many he had. He had cows he'd never even seen before. He was forever trying to catch them and put tags in their ears. He had started with two cows in 1949 and now he had around four or five hundred head, and they intermingled and bred unchecked and ran more or less wild on his place, through woods and pastures and a river bottom.

I showed up at his house wearing cowboy boots, jeans, and a long-sleeved shirt. My uncle had learned to rope and ride cutting horses after the war and he had taught me how. He had a brown gelding named Thunderbolt, who was aptly named. Riding him was like riding a fifteen-hundred-pound jackrabbit. He could start so fast that he could slide you backwards out of the saddle and then make a turn and bounce you off his hip as he was leaving. I had learned to ride him at first by holding onto the horn with both hands. And then I had learned to move with the horse. He was worth $18,000.

My uncle came out of the house. Thunderbolt and another horse were standing saddled in the yard.

"Why don't you write a western?" he said. "I bet you could sell a western."

"I don't want to write westerns."

"I bet you could sell one, though."

He pointed to Thunderbolt and I climbed up on him. He got on the other horse and we left through the gate. We kicked them a little and then cantered down through the pasture with the wind in our hair. The cows that had been standing in the bottom suddenly raised their tails like deer and took off running. The horses' hooves drummed in the earth. Clods of black dirt and grass were torn loose and kicked into the air behind us. Uncle Lou started swinging his rope. Most of the cows had horns, and some had Brahma blood. All of them were heavy and muscular and mean-tempered.

162

What I would have given for my little boy to be in the saddle with me.

We cut a couple of cows out from the main group and raced along beside them. We gradually singled one out, a long lean gray cow with sharp tapering horns. I had to make a loop wide enough to settle over her head. I stood in the stirrups with the running end of the rope in my teeth and whirled the loop over my head and leaned forward and dropped it over her horns. I snubbed it tight on the saddle horn and Thunderbolt put on the brakes. When the cow hit the end of the rope, she went tail over head and hit the ground flat on her back, all the wind knocked out of her. Uncle Lou roped a hind foot and we got off the horses while they stood with their backs arched and holding her tight, and we wrapped two of her feet together with a pigging string. We took the ropes off her horns and the hind foot, and left her on the ground, bawling, with her eyes rolled up white in her head with anger. Then we coiled our ropes and took off after another one.

My uncle had been with a boy from Montana in the war. He had become close friends with this boy and after the war was over the boy invited him to come and stay with him and his family for a while. My uncle wasn't married, and didn't have anything at home to hold him or draw him back with any immediacy, so he went. The boy's family had a ranch high in the mountains, and they had been punching cows for four generations. My uncle didn't know which end of a horse was which, but they taught him. They taught him how to rope and brand and bulldog and bullride and even cook. They taught him how to hunt elk and how to rig packsaddles. They took him in like another son, fed him and washed his clothes. My uncle in turn had showed me some of these things. The thing unsaid that was hurting him the most was knowing that now he might not get to do it for my kids.

We didn't talk while we worked. We flushed the cows from the woods like coveys of quail, and then he pointed to a brutish-looking cow that was trotting away rapidly through some sage grass, watching us over her shoulder. She had some truly wicked horns. I wouldn't have gone after her. Uncle Lou rode straight for her. I let Thunderbolt get too close. He put his shoulder against her rump, and she whirled and opened a five-inch cut in his shoulder with her horn. Uncle Lou snatched a 30.30 Marlin from a scabbard on his saddle and shot the cow dead between the eyes and hollered that he'd dress the motherfucker later. Blood poured down Thunderbolt's leg. The lips of the wound were flapping, open and loose. I could see the muscle beneath it bunching and working. These were the things I had done to my uncle with the circumstances of my own life, my divorce, my writing. I had cost him money and pain in a way that was no fault of his whatsoever. We kept riding. Thunderbolt bore it silently. We roped another cow. I kept working somehow. The day was long and I knew that other days would be long, and I knew that men sometimes had to be close to other men to help them through the hard times. Because that's what these times were.

14

We stood outside in the dust of the New Albany stockyard. The smell of shit was overpowering. Nobody was being murdered yet, they were just now getting sold. It made me a little sick, but how else could I enjoy my juicy T-bones if not some cattle took the big one in the brain? I tried not to think about them being hoisted, throats cut, skinned, sawed up. Ground up. Once in a while a little piece of rebellious bone from a long-dead cow would rise up in my mouth from the hamburger meat at Kroger's and threaten to chip a tooth. *Revenge of the Cows*. Let's don't make a movie out of it.

Lots of guys around there had cowboy boots on. Some had barrel chests and bellies and checkered shirts. I felt somehow inferior and unmanly in the midst of them, even though plenty of shit was smeared on my own boots. I leaned, if not physically, at least spiritually in the direction of my uncle, who was at peace there, at one with his own kind. Which I certainly didn't have anything against.

We had our cow tickets and we perched up on the corral above the auction ring.

Obba deebe mobba beebe forty mouth a poe,
Six potater sebm potater fo potater moe,
I'm a tater you a tater kick him out the doe.
Hummmbabe who gonna gimme ten gimme ten ten
   gimme Rin Tin Tin;
Humbabe well you wanna watch this cow on the flo,
Hooma jimmy homma fimmy moe.

It went on like that for a while. I admired the auctioneers.
They wore straw hats and were good old boys. They had big,
round voices. I hated it that I had a scratchy, raspy voice, the
kind of voice that made me sick when I taped it along with
"Top Forty Hits" and listened to it late at night, singing songs
like "Puff the Magic Dragon" and "Blowin' in the Wind." I
had a small cheap guitar I tried to play when I couldn't write,
with twangy strings, but I only knew four chords, G, C, D,
and G7. I had once made the mistake of making a tape of
myself playing and singing George Jones's "Yabba Dabba Do,
The King Is Gone, And So Are You," and leaving it lying
around. Marilyn had played part of it, much to the amuse-
ment of some guests at a party at our house one night, while
I was in the kitchen mixing drinks and boiling shrimp, and it
hadn't endeared her to me to walk in and realize what was
going on, people sniggering, and so on.

First thing they did was run two shoat pigs out into the
ring. First thing one of the pigs did was leap through the pipe
bars and shit in a man's lap. The man was trying to get up out
of his chair, and he was holding the pig while it was shitting
on him. Later on the man bought the pig, I was sure just so
he could kill it. But the pig wouldn't understand. I've heard
that pigs are very smart. Pigs learn how to hunt truffles. A
pig in Arkansas was trained to point birds once. I believe pigs
contributed to Ulysses' downfall. I've eaten a lot of pork chops
myself. Imagine the pigs that have to die for us. These pigs
go valiantly not even to their graves; they don't even have any
graves, when you think about it. You ever seen a pig graveyard? What would you put on his tombstone?

Here lies no pig;
Don't dig.
Ain't no bones,
Just leave em alone.

Some horses ran through, got sold pretty fast. I had eyes
for a Mexican-looking señorita who was selling sandwiches. I
ate two pork barbecues and then realized that the pigs had
probably come through the ring a few weeks before, pigs
without a future, pigs without a life insurance plan. Pigs
who'd never been set down around the supper table and
oinked to. Pigs who just didn't know how good they'd had it,
plenty of mud and corn to wallow among, happy days over
with now.

She seemed to be a señorita, but I didn't know for sure. I
was still thinking about Betti Del Oreo. I decided I would
write her a real nice letter.

15

Dear Miss DeLoreo,
Thanks for taking so much time to tell me why the story
was rejected. Most editors wouldn't do that. It's pretty
lonely out here, you know, writing all these things and
not getting anybody to pay any attention to them. I
appreciate you taking the time, though. I'm gonna try to
write something better for you. Something that'll make
you stand up and put the gloves on with them.

Best wishes,
Leon Barlow

I was nervous as hell when I mailed the letter. I don't know why. I didn't even know her. And maybe she was seventy years old, retired from Florida or something, with skinny knees. But why couldn't she be some *goddess*, kneeling in the streets of New York for the right prophet to come along? With the rain in her face, black hair beautiful, screaming for me?

I licked it shut and sent it. I'd enclosed a story, also.

I was waiting for the check from my uncle for the two cows he'd given me that we'd subsequently sold. The other cow, the one he'd shot for goring Thunderbolt, was probably down in the pasture still, stinking, covered with flies, coyotes eating on it, but I didn't want to go check. There were some things I didn't want to be around and rotting putrid meat was one of them.

16

I smoked some marijuana and drank a lot of beer one day and then wrote this:

HONED

Honed's daddy had a good reason for changing his name early. But he was almost too late with the thought. He had Honed up in his arms, wrapped in a nice soft blanket Honed's mother had spent about eight and a half months knitting, with little flowers and soft bunny rabbits hopping around on it in fields of green clover—real nice stuff for a kid they'd just gotten to know—just pure damn love for the little guy—and he'd been kissing around on Honed's head and telling his koochie-poo that MomMom was right behind them in a wheelchair and so *he* was going to warm his bottles and stuff for him for a while, since MomMom had had her puss stretched inside out. But Honed didn't have any idea what was happening. They'd had to calm him down anyway. He was upset big time. He'd been rudely expulsed from the warm dark saltwater sea of his mother's belly, where he'd begun to think he'd always be, into the hard red hands of a grinning bald-headed guy with big white teeth (Like fangs! Shit! Honed thought) who hit him on the ass four or five times. And then a whole bunch of people he didn't even know had been dressing him and undressing him and they even messed with his goober for a while one day —there was still something going on down there but he was scared to look (I've got to figure out what the hell's going on, he thought)—so he was just mainly trying to sleep and hide from it all he could. He knew that he was helpless and at their mercy. He couldn't walk, couldn't talk, couldn't do anything but shit and cry. And they were all a lot bigger than he was.

Honed's daddy named him Ned originally. And it occurred to him just as he was going down the hall with Honed in his arms, getting ready to take him home, that people would be saying Hi to Ned a lot in his life (which he hoped would run about a hundred wonderful years) and where they were going home to, they wouldn't necessarily say Hi. They might say Hey. But a bunch of them would probably say Ho. Ho Ned. Whassup, main? And then when Ned came up in his world and put his legs into his britches like men do, he'd be out in it seeing people. If they said Hi they'd say Hined and if they said Ho they'd say Honed. (He was a little whacky, Honed's daddy. But he didn't live long after Honed was born anyway. And he was a good guy. He could have done a lot for Honed. He was a millionaire playboy/professor with two published novels, and the MacArthur Foundation was getting ready to give him about $60,000 a year for five years when he got killed. It actually happened in a freight elevator. It was very ironical. It was at the very top of the Empire State Building, when it was still the tallest. Honed's daddy was the kind of brilliant person who is severely dumb in other ways. He mistook the freight elevator for the one people were supposed to ride. He rode it all right. He punched floor seven, and what they thought happened was all the relays that controlled the up cables blew, and the damn thing just took off, straight up, flying. Honed's daddy peed all over himself. It was a horrible death. And he knew he was going to die. That was the thing. He did have enough sense to know that it was going up way too fast, the floors just flashing by on the lights. But he was calm even in the face of that. He allowed himself three-quarters of a second of all-out, mindless mute screaming-ass terror, and then dropped his briefcase and started punching elevator buttons. Nothing happened. A bunch of mechanical things that the elevator people *should have been maintaining a little more closely* gave way at the same time. Oh, they had a big lawsuit, and Honed's mother got richer than she already was, but it didn't bring Honed's daddy back. The elevator car hit the top of its channel with so much force that it threw Honed's daddy up against the ceiling of the car and broke open a big place in his head. One cable snapped on impact, and the motor downstairs started freewheeling without belts because they had snapped, too, and the other cable was strong enough almost to hold the car all those hundreds and hundreds of feet above the floor of New York City. But then it snapped, too. Honed's daddy was on the floor, stretched out, his eyes closed, his fingers trying to dig. The downward rush was so great that Honed's daddy's body was actually floating about an inch above the floor of the car a millisecond before it hit the basement.) What Honed's daddy thought, standing just short of the doors of the hospital with Honed in his arms, was that he would save all those people the trouble of saying Ho, comma, Ned, and call him Honed. And in that way be kind of like a tribute to Honed for someone to say his name. That kind of thinking may be crazy, but that's the kind of thinking Honed's daddy did.

I never finished that one, either.

17

The check from my uncle came in the mail. It was $1143.68, and it was made out to me. I booked. Salad tomatoes, some movies, couple of cassettes, shrimp, some oysters, couple of sirloins, beer, whiskey, some blue jeans, a belt, two shirts, some underwear, some Collins mix, garbage bags, a broom, Spic 'n' Span, a cigarette lighter, *The Sound and the Fury*, *Hot Water Music*, *Jujitsu for Christ*, *Child of God*, *The Complete Stories of Flannery O'Connor*, *The Old Man and the Sea*, some barbecue bread, socks, a *TV Guide*, fourteen typewriter ribbons, some of those little chocolate-covered cherries, some kids' clothes, a little blue squeeze giraffe that squeaked when you squeezed it, a little baseball and bat and glove, some rubbers, some toothpaste, some English Leather, some fingernail clippers, some shampoo, Slim Jims, barbecued pigskins, some Jimmy Dean smoked sausage, catfish, some seafood sauce, two reams of paper, some correction film, four dozen manila envelopes, some ink pens, a new *Writer's Market*, a new band for my wristwatch, some rolling papers, a fanbelt, some brake shoes, a sending unit for my oil pressure gauge, G and A guitar strings, and some charcoal.

It was kind of like Christmas.

I hauled all that home, called my ex-wife and told her I had some stuff for the kids she could pick up at my mother's, told her I was fixing to write her lawyer a check for two months' alimony, hung up, sat down, wrote the check, addressed an envelope, considered writing him a letter, didn't, licked it shut, put a stamp on it that I steamed off one of my returned envelopes that the postal employees had let edge through the cancelling machine, and walked down the driveway whistling and put it in the mailbox.

When I stepped back in the house there was still some of the money left. Provisions had been laid in. I was ready for the siege. I opened a beer, took a swig, put on Johann Pachelbel's Kanon and listened. My uncle had caused all this. And he was out three cows over it. Later that night I called him and thanked him, and tried to explain the enormity of what he had done for me, how he had given me at least sixty days of freedom and time to write, but all he said was don't mention it.

18

Couple of days later it was her on the phone. I asked her if she'd gotten her mon.

"Yeah, I got it. Where'd you get it?"

"That's all right where I got it. You don't need to call over here and get nasty with me just because I made your alimony payment on time."

"I ain't being nasty with you. I know where you got it anyway."

"You don't neither."

"I bet I do."

"No, you don't."

"Yes, I do."

"Don't do it."

"Do too."

"Well, where'd I get it, then, you know so much?"

"Your uncle gave it to you. He sold two cows and gave you the money."

"Who told you that?"

"Your mother."

"Goddamn it."

"She tells me everything."

"I bet by God she won't after I get through talking to her."

"What you so pissed about? I got a right to know what you're doing."

"Not any more you don't."

"Did you make it home all right that night?"

"What night?"

"That night I talked to you. I don't guess you remember it, you's so drunk. Couldn't hardly walk. You gonna have a car wreck and kill yourself one night. Or fuck some old haint and get AIDS all over you. Then what's your kids gonna do for a daddy?"

"I wasn't aware that they had one now other than biologically speaking."

"Other than biologically speaking? You are so full of shit, Leon, do you know that?"

"Are you through bending my ear? Cause if you ain't, tough shit. I'm through talking to you. I got your damn alimony paid so I don't want to hear another word out of you for two months. You got that?"

"Sure. Less one of the kids gets sick or something."

"Yeah. Well, call me if that happens. I want to know if they're sick."

"I mean to pay the bills. You got to pay the doctor bills, too, you know."

"I *know*, Marilyn. Now anything else? No? Bye!"

Fuck you. Goddamn couldn't write while I was married to you and now I'm having to listen to you while I'm divorced, trying to work over here. Shit. Get me so goddamn upset I can't even do anything for thinking about all the shit you get me upset about. Call over here and mess up a whole day's work because of you. Didn't even mention the stuff I got the kids. Just wanted to worry the hell out of me for a while. Probably told them you bought it yourself. Be just like you.

19

I wondered if the great Betti DeLoreo would write me back. I wondered how high up she was. It was entirely possible that she might be fat, fifty-eight, and gap-toothed. She was probably married and had grown children. She might be bulimic, or lesbian, or have no legs. What did I mean imagining these things about people I didn't even know? I did it, though. I imagined what she looked like. I imagined her flying down from New York and pulling up outside in a white stretch limo and getting out, flashing a lot of leg, telling the driver to wait, coming in, Leon? Yes, Leon darling, yes, and then pulling off her fur and having this cleavage like Jayne Mansfield. I actually sat at the typewriter and did that. I did that a lot. Usually while I was under the influence of Uncle Bud.

20

I got drunk one night. Actually several nights in a row and it scared me. When I came to, I believed I had been on a "running drunk" for two days. It was the first time that had ever happened to me, and I'd always said it never would. Now I had done it, and it hadn't seemed that hard.

I curled up there in my bed the next morning and thought about it. This is what brought it on. You've got your art and you've got your precious life and where does that leave room for them? I rolled over, closed my eyes, mashed my face into that pillow. Trying to keep that old sickening straight truth from pushing in. If you's worth a shit you'd act right. Stay home two or *three* nights a week anyway. You just love to run drunk. Ain't nothing going to help it. You can fix it for a while and then it's all going to come back. Sooner or later. You can straighten up for a while till things get better and then gradually you'll get off into it again. Why she left you. Look how long she stayed. And you just threw it all away. Think about those fat little faces. That little one cutting teeth, crawling, whatever. You a sorry son of a bitch. Probably don't even know how old they are. Yeah . . . Alisha's . . . twenty-one months . . . Alan's four years three months.

I sat up in the bed. Had the sheet up over my legs, like I was going to get up with it wrapped around me like guys you see in these TV movies or even real movies where they don't want their dicks to be seen, but it's really ironical when you think about it, like two people who have been slamming each other's bodies naked for two hours are suddenly going to get up and wrap sheets around them.

Yeah, I was sorry. Sorry as hell. Sorriest sumbitch ever shit behind a pair of shoes. But one thing in my favor was that I wouldn't rather climb a tree and tell you a lie than stand on the ground and tell you the truth. No sir, you could trust me to do what I said. I had a lot of things wrong with me, but lying wasn't one of them.

That old sunshine was burning in on my head. I had a bunch of pimples on my legs, or maybe not pimples, just these little red irritated spots from wearing long pants all my life. Man wasn't meant to wear long pants, but my legs are so skinny I can hardly bear it.

It was hot as hell. Again. My head was hurting, and I had

about two truckloads of guilt on me. They'd already backed up and dumped. Right on my head.

The day didn't seem worth getting dressed for. So I flopped again.

21

It was hotter than before when I woke. Sweat had matted the hair on the side of my head. The pillow was damp with it. It seemed to be about two o'clock in the afternoon. I knew the mail had run.

I lay there and thought about it. What good would it do to get up and go see? The motherfuckers weren't going to publish any of it.

I got up and showered. I looked out the window. My neighbor's corn in the field next door was being burnt, parched, withered. He was having a rough time of it, too.

I went down and checked the mail. Water bill, light bill, phone bill, and somebody wanting to give me an AM/FM radio worth $39.95 if I bought a quarter acre of land in some resort area in Arkansas for $6800. Nothing from Betti De-Loreo. But at least nothing had come back. Yet. I had fourteen stories on their way to or back from various editorial offices across America.

I went back to the house, opened a beer, and sat down at the machine. I sat there all afternoon waiting for it to say something to me, and it never did.

22

I wanted to write a story about love one morning. I liked love and could hardly do without it, but I didn't really want to write a love story. I mean not a bodice-ripper. So I started writing a story about a lady whose husband had died and left her with two children. He had been killed in a tragic pulpwood-cutting accident, mashed flat by a falling pine tree, and now he was dead and gone, fresh dirt heaped over his grave. The lady, whose name was suddenly Marie, couldn't even afford to buy him a headstone. He, the lately deceased husband, who didn't need a name, had not taken out a large life insurance policy to provide for his family's future in the event of a sudden and unexpected death. As a matter of fact, one night after a long day of pulpwood cutting only two weeks before, he had told an insurance salesman who had come by to see him that he didn't have time to listen to that shit, and would he get the fuck out the door. Two weeks later, pow. Flat as a pancake. The kids were grabbing hold of the doorknobs hollering Biscuit, Daddy, biscuit. Marie didn't have any skills, couldn't read. Plus she had a nervous condition that made her head shake very slightly. She didn't know what she was going to do, how she was going to provide for these two children, who needed Pampers and other things.

She tried go-go dancing for three nights, locking her sleeping children in the car in the parking lot. But it was no good. She couldn't concentrate on her rhythm, thinking about the kids outside, whether they were awake or not, crying, thinking they had been abandoned. So she had to turn in her

G-string. She drove home through the night, gripping the steering wheel "so tightly her knuckles whitened,," wondering what she was going to do. The kids continued to sleep in the back seat, secure in the knowledge that their mother would take care of them.

Marie rode around for a while, wondering why her husband hadn't had enough sense to buy life insurance. She didn't even have dog food for their dog.

At this point I realized I couldn't help them, realized I wasn't a writer, and threw it away, which scared the shit out of me.

23

I was sitting on the porch drinking a beer about sundown. Nothing was good. My life was rotten. My ex-wife would have a yoke around my neck for the rest of my life, and if I happened to remarry one day, her hate would be doubled. I didn't know if I could take double hate. Nothing I could ever do would be able to repair the feelings that had been stomped on. I had promised before God in His church to cherish her always and I had not honored that promise.

I heard a car turning in the driveway, saw headlamps coming up even though it was too early for them. It was Monroe. The evening gloam was upon us. It was gloaming time. We would be Gloamriders in the Sky.

He shut off the motor and got out with a beer, stuck his arm back in and turned off the lights. He got up on the porch and sat down beside me in a chair.

"What's up, man?" he said.

"Not much. Just sitting here watching it get dark."

"You want a beer?"

"I've got one. You need one?"

"I've got one. You want to go ride around?"

"Suits me. Let me get some more beer."

"I've got plenty. Just come on and get in."

I got in. We rode down the road.

"What do you hear from your old lady?" he said.

"That she hates my guts."

"That's nothing new, is it?"

"No."

We rode for a while. Drank a while. He had some Thin Lizzy and he plugged old Philip Lynott in and the evening gloam began to turn purple and be immersed with beautiful gray-lit white clouds that rolled high up in the heavens and began to slowly unfold like gigantic marshmallows or mushrooms until the beauty of it just made me shake my head. I was alive, he was alive, the snakes were in the ditches, the deer were beginning to ease out of the woods, the beer was cold, he was free from his old lady, I was free from my old lady, both of us were just free as birds. We'd both been through the woman trouble and we knew what it was. It was a heartsick and a fuckup and nobody could warn you from one to the next. Lose one, get another one. One day loves you and then another day years apart hates you. You bastard. You sorry son of a bitch. Oh yes, baby, do it make me *come*. All them words out of the same mouth. Tsk, tsk. Be my *only* baby. Get up and fix it yourself.

"We in the gloam, old buddy," he said. "We definitely right in the middle of it."

It was true. James Street had given us the phraseology. The wind was sweeping our hair. We had the windows rolled down, arms stuck out. It was warm. Life was alive, and real, and we were not putting a whole lot of poisonous emissions into the air. I felt about as good as I'd felt in a while.

"It's a gloaming, all right," I said.

He kind of snickered over there at the steering wheel.

"Let's go fuck up. You want to?"

"Fuck up? Where at?"

"Ah hell, we can just go fuck up uptown if you want to. I don't care. Just anywhere."

I lit me a cigarette. I'd been cutting down.

"Ah hell. I don't guess I better go fuck up. I think we fucked up a lot the last two nights, didn't we?"

"In a row, buddy roe. In a row. That's why I want to get out so bad and fuck up tonight. See if we can't make it three in a row."

"Boy, I was fucked up last night."

"I know it. I was, too. Do you remember us even going home?"

"Naw, man. I was too fucked up."

We rode some more. The stars couldn't make it out yet, not yet, but they'd be peeking before long. Night was going to cover the land. Everything that slept in the woods would wake up then, the coons from their lairs and the rabbits that feared everything. I could almost see the beavers' heads cutting the ripples up Potlockney Creek. I wanted woman-flesh. I mean, as good as that was, I wanted long hair in my hands, and breasts on my chest. And I was aching, awful, didn't want him to see. So I said: "Yeah. All right. Let's go fuck up."

24

We woke up hot. Out in the middle of the woods. Why we do these things I don't know. It seems so easy when you first start out. Couple of cold beers, little smoke. Ain't going to hurt nothing or nobody. Just going to pass off an enjoyable evening. And wind up almost dying before you get home.

He wasn't in the car. He was out on the ground. Lying in a patch of sunlight with ticks crawling all over him. It was nine o'clock. He was fucked for work. And would have to call in.

Bark and stuff were stuck to his face when I woke him up. He couldn't believe where we were. We'd had no nooky, neither of us. The nooky was all at home asleep. We had some vomit dried on us, real regular pickup guys. Swinging Singles. We were as bad a fuckup as a screen door in a submarine.

He didn't want to get up. Wanted to just stay there on the ground and sleep. Said he could make it if I just moved him into the shade.

25

I was sitting on the back porch the next evening not doing a damn thing. Drinking a beer. I'd said fuck it for the day. I'd hammered some stuff out, but I didn't know for sure how good it was. It felt good, but I wasn't certain. The world at large had a pretty narrow-minded conception of everything. Some rootintooter from Chillicothe might get ahold of my stuff, and not have on his favorite pair of crotchless panties that day, and that might cause him to reject my work. I didn't know. I knew editors had to be human, but I also knew that some of them had to be square, uncool, unreceptive to cool new work. I also knew that plenty of them were actively looking for the next new voice. I just didn't know how to find them. They didn't have names that I knew, and the names they had, I didn't know how to find.

It looked like a bat uprising out there. Like all the bats in all the caves of hell had decided to come out and fly around my house. I grew tired of it pretty quickly. I got my shotgun and started shucking and pumping. Pow! Blow your little ass out of the sky. Blam! Leave a hole for the moon to look through.

Well, I harried them away from the dusk, finally. Blew a couple of holes in a few flocks. How could they hang upside down and sleep? I didn't care, because I wasn't with Marilyn any more, and Betti DeLoreo hadn't answered, and I had about four beers in me, which seems to be the break point for me, when I make the decision to fuck up or not. Usually I do, but to my credit, there have been a few times when I have not.

26

Same evening, a little later, I'd moved the speakers out onto the back porch and I was communing with nature a little. I loved nature and I felt like nature loved me. Why else would they send those fireflies, and doves, and geese that honked like a pack of wild dogs howling down the sky?

Dark was fine with me. That was when the women moved. They were sort of like snakes, or owls, looking to see what they could latch onto in the night. I loved them for that, thought it was a fine way to be. That was the way I was, and I didn't figure anything was going to change it.

I heard him slowing down on the highway before he got close to the driveway. The distant roaring grew slighter; he was giving himself plenty of room to slow down, taking it easy on his brake shoes. I looked out across the trees and the river and the grass. Catfish were swimming down there in the water. Old turtles that were there when Lee surrendered. I'd seen them, monsters with moss on their heads, pulled up from the depths and clawing against the boat. If you sit down there in a boat still enough, the beavers will come out and sit on the banks and wash their hands and faces.

Yeah, it looked like a night for women. He kept slowing down, coming nearer, and I cranked it up just a little on Thin Lizzy's "Cowboy Song." I hated it that Philip was dead, and it had only been a couple of weeks since Roy Orbison had died. My heroes had fallen all around me, had been falling for years. Hendrix and Morrison and Joplin and Croce and Chapin and Redding, Elvis and Sam Cooke, he was dead, too, Lennon and Mama Cass, I didn't even want to think about the rest of them.

I heard the gravel crunching under his wheels. Coming to take me away. Lights lanced around the side of the house. I heard his alternator protesting a loose belt, and all fell to naught. I sipped my beer. I'd been sipping beer for a couple of hours, waiting on him.

27

The girl looked dead. Damn, she's dead, I thought, looking at her. But then I looked at Monroe and thought, Surely to God he's not dead, too. Finally I could see their chests rising and falling. His pants were halfway on, hers were halfway off. The sun was on us again. We were sort of like superstrong vampires who just got sickened by the sun. It wasn't going to kill us or anything. But it sure didn't make us feel good at certain times.

They were on the back seat. I was on the front. Somebody was plowing a field on a tractor right across the road from us. It was pretty unwonderful there, and to wonder who else might ought to be with us and where we might have left them and what stages of jail/bail we might have left them in, since I vaguely remembered us having some running mates with us at some point the night before.

I woke them up. Monroe seemed to think that a couple of them might be in the Pontotoc County jail and need our renderings, slim as they were.

We booked, naturally, to the Pontotoc County jail. A large man with red cheeks presented himself at the front door.

"Hep y'all?"

"Yessir, we think we got some friends in jail over here maybe."

"Name?"

"What's their names, Monroe?"

She spoke up. "Jerome and Kerwood White." She was look-ing sort of anxious, since they were her little brothers.

"White? White. I don't believe I've got them names on my list. Now I believe we had two Whites killed in a car wreck last night. Here it is. Yeah. That them? Jerome and Kerwood? One subjeck twenty-seven, one twenty-five. Dead on impact. Tractor trailer over here on Highway 6. Cut one of em's head off, I believe. Y'all some kin to the family?"

28

The funeral of those boys was not a good place to be. It was raining, and muddy, and people were beating each other with fists of grief and screaming and blaming the whole thing on God. It was ironic since they'd all come to Him for comfort on this particular day. I saw some lady bust her ass on the church steps, had black bikini panties on, showed it to the whole world. I had several cuts on my head that nobody could explain.

The place where they buried them was down under a hill with white oak trees. It was very muddy. You could see it sticking to the heels of the ladies' shoes. It was that red clay that lifts out two shoe sizes when you raise your foot. But what made me sadder than anything was all the old wreaths and styrofoam green spray-painted crosses from old monu-ments and tributes to love piled up against a rusty barbed-wire fence, forlorn and all, wet, funky. Funky funky love. I realized right that moment how different were the different types of love. Love between man and woman, husband and wife, was much different from, say, between son and father, or father and daughter, or brother and sister, or brother and brother, and father-in-law to second cousin. Love for the right person could make you do anything, give up your own life. I knew there was love that strong. I felt it for my children. I looked next to me and saw Jerome and Kerwood White's mama and daddy holding each other up, staring at those two coffins, and I thought of times in diapers and even before, dates and weddings and visits on the front porch, the first kiss, a little house to start with until some kids came along. What they had on their faces was horror.

I was afraid I knew how it would go. He'd start drinking more, and she'd age quickly. From her loneliness and grief. There'd be a hole in her that nobody'd be able to fill up. Sex at their age was probably not much of a consideration any more. But maybe it was, between them. I hoped it was. I hoped it was an intimate thing between them that would hold them together, his wrinkled old body naked up against her old wrinkled naked body, bodies they remembered from forty years ago. But if it didn't . . . if that couldn't hold them together . . . if there were late nights home from the bars . . . her knitting in the living room, so quiet . . . what purpose to their lives any more. Two of the things they had centered on for so long. From diapers to death. And probably drunk when they died.

I went over to them and held them. I cried with them. They didn't know me. They cried with me anyway.

29

I saw Raoul's poem. It appeared in the spring issue of *Rabbe Mabbe*. They'd edited it a little, toned it down, taken some or most of the guts out of it, but Raoul didn't want to talk about it. He was writing a novel. I said Go for it, motherfucker.

30

I got the kids one weekend and she went off to spend it with somebody, I don't know if it was male or female. At that point I wouldn't have put anything past her. I just hoped she wasn't doing anything adverse around the kids.

Alisha shit on me a couple of times. Alan and I built a big fire in the back yard out of wood crates and things and roasted twenty-seven hot dogs and a pack of marshmallows. We pitched our old tent and carried quilts out of the house and pillows and camped out in the back yard the whole weekend except for TV-watching inside in the daytime. Alisha liked it. We didn't know if she was retarded or not. There was a chance, they said, but we didn't know yet. She seemed slow. Slow to focus her eyes, slow to understand words. Slow to learn to use the pot.

At night in the tent I held her to my chest and felt her heart beating under her skin, felt the silk of her hair brushing against my face. You deserve better parents than us, kiddo, I thought. She would try to talk but the words would never come. I must have said Daddy to her five hundred times that weekend, just trying to get her to say it. She never would.

But she knew who Daddy was. That was the main thing. She might not have had that word in her head. But she knew who Daddy was.

Alan did, too. He was my cowboy. I wanted him on Thunderbolt with me and I told myself I'd call Uncle Lou about it. We all slept in one sleeping bag because I wanted them close to me, I wanted their little faces and their little hands on me and I wanted to breathe their little sweet untainted exhalations all night long. I did that. And on Sunday evening at five o'clock I gave them back to their mother and tried not to cry when they went down the driveway, waving back to me through the glass and the dust.

31

Monroe blamed himself for those boys' deaths. That girl was their sister, but I hadn't known that earlier. What they'd done was drive their car at ninety miles an hour under a tractor-trailer that was crossing the highway. One skid mark was ninety feet long. The Highway Patrol said that meant they had one brake shoe working. They went 302 feet out the other side of it before coasting to a rest. The entire top was one small pinched thing like a steel suitcase.

I had to go over to the junkyard with them and look at it. Their sister cried softly on Monroe's shoulder the whole time. I didn't know what had happened, didn't know that we'd met them and gotten in with them briefly and rode around with them for a while, and then gone back to our cars and let them go on to their deaths. She seemed to think somehow that it was all my fault. I hadn't even been driving.

I told them I'd see them later.

32

Marilyn called me again. Betti DeLoreo hadn't answered yet. I was getting pretty impatient. I wanted to know the news whether it was good or bad. I didn't mind screwing around with uncertainty, it was dead flat failure I had a problem with.

"Lisha's got ticks all over her."

"We had her out in the tent. Put some nail polish on em. What are they? Those little bitty ticks?"

"Yeah. Them little tiny ones. You can't hardly see em."

"They don't carry tick fever. That's the Spotted Brown Dog Tick."

"What are you doing?"

"Nothing. Trying to write. Enjoying knowing you can't even think about trying to wring my balls for thirty-eight more days."

"Well. I'm getting to be pretty good friends with Judge Johnson. He bought me a milkshake down at Burger King the other day."

"He sounds like a real groovy guy."

"Oh, he is, he is. He thinks it's a shame how divorced women get treated in Missippi."

"What is he, a liberal?"

"I think he's horny."

"He probably is. I guess you been shaking your ass at him."

"Nah."

"Don't tell me. You let him look down your shirt."

"I think I'm fixing to change jobs."

"Oh yeah?"

"Yeah."

"I heard about a good job the other day."

"You did?"

"Yeah."

"Where is it?"

"Up at a woodworking mill in Memphis. They need somebody to eat sawdust and shit two-by-fours. You interested?"

"I'm gonna have you begging for mercy."

"Not me, baby."

"You wait and see. You going out with anybody?"

"I wouldn't tell you if I was."

"What, she some great old big fat thing with great big titties?"

"Wouldn't you like to know?"

"Well. I been dating a guy that's *real* nice. And for your information, he thought *Blue Velvet* was a sick movie."

"Shit. What'd you do, rent it just so you could see if he thought it was a sick movie?"

"No."

"Boy. I bet David Lynch is just losing his lunch right now because you and your boyfriend thought his movie was sick. You dilbert-head."

"Well, that wasn't the only thing you were crazy over. Anybody who'd buy a red hunting hat and turn it around backwards on his head, and wear it like that, get up in the bathroom and tap dance . . ."

"Look. We've been over this time and time again. He wasn't crazy."

"Then why'd they put him in that place?"

"Because they *thought* he was crazy."

"Aha! See there!"

"Look, goddamnit. For the last time. His little brother died. This kid he knew jumped out a window and killed himself. And he was just a kid himself. Now if you don't think that would fuck somebody up . . ."

"But it was just a book!"

I paused.

"Right, right," I said, and eased the receiver gently onto the cradle.

33

Some more stories came back in. Some had marvelous rejection slips. Nobody promised their body to me over any of them. I knew that would come later. But I wished they'd hurry up. I still hadn't legged down with anybody and I knew that my sperm was backed up pretty deep. I didn't want the heartbreak of prostate trouble.

I tried to write all I could. I tried to put balls and heart and blood into it like a good writer had once told me to do. Sometimes it wasted me, just laid me out. I knew that at least some of what I was writing was good, but I just hadn't found anybody to share my vision yet. Nobody with any power. Nobody who could say yes or no to publication. I knew about the pecking order, and jealousy, and interdepartmental office memos and the little notes that were jotted with a quick hand. They didn't know about the careers they were advancing or retarding with their little papers, the numbers of us who lived and died with a stroke of their pens. They didn't have any idea of the power they wielded. We were a vast unfaced effluvium of authors with unproven work, and there was so much bad that it was hard to find the good in all of it. Maybe they became jaded with it, their eyes turned to stone by the shit that fell before them. Maybe so much bad work had convinced them that it all looked alike, that nothing was going to come from the shit pile, that the quest was already over and they weren't going to discover the next Hemingway. I felt these things strongly. I couldn't prove them, but I felt them.

I wondered if the great Betti DeLoreo was somewhere in her high ivory tower, her fingernails painted red, her black mane of hair drawn to one side, reading manuscripts, one load of shit after another. I wondered if she was thinking of me. I knew the chance was small. There were many of us and only one of her. And she was only one cog in a big machine. It seemed almost hopeless sometimes, but I knew I had to keep going on. I had chosen my own path. Nothing could turn me from it.

34

I was in a bar one night and I had been drinking before I got there. I knew I was treading on shaky ground, drinking at night in town and then having to drive myself home. The state troopers nailed people with regularity. It helped to take

secondary roads, to be responsible. I had good intentions that
were often spoiled by drinking.

The evenings began it. The two or three beers in the late
evening, then the false sense of security when night fell. To
be driving on the backroads, the cooler in the floorboard.
Little music playing. The road just slowly going by at thirty-
five miles an hour. But sometimes the road wound to town.

Sometimes you see somebody you don't like and you know
when you look at him that the feeling is mutual. Your eyes
meet briefly and then part, like two dogs sizing each other
up. And any time later that night when you look at him, he'll
be looking at you. You only have to wait for the liquor to do its
work to get your surprise. Your mouthful of fist, if it comes.

That was what I happened to be facing that night. Some
fucker with a freaky face. I guess he was jealous of my hand-
some one, or relatively unmarked one anyway, which was the
main difference between us. First off, somebody'd kicked both
his front teeth out. And then bit off half of one of his ears.
Then they, like, tried to *gouge* his right eye out with a class
ring or something, really grinding it deep into the tissue of
his eyelid, so that it hung down halfway over the eye and gave
him this . . . freaky look. Man has a problem. You understand
it immediately. He won't go to a plastic surgeon. Whatever in
his life led him to his altered state won't let him repair himself.
He'd rather take it out on unscarred people like you, try to
make you look more like him. It's the kind of thing that makes
you want to turn your back and finish your beer and find
another place to drink in that night. Because after he's given
you that pit bull look, you know you won't go unchallenged.

I knew a few people down there shooting pool. They had some peeled cedar posts propping the ceiling up. Playmates were plastered over the same ceiling. You could look up and see titties of the most delectable types. Small rounded asses reclining over velvet couches, their elegant legs stretched out. Where do they find these women? They're not out here in the world. I've never seen them. They don't hang out in this particular bar, anyway.

I just moseyed around for a while. It was really pretty dull. I should have been at home writing. But I'd written so much I was temporarily tired of it. And I was hoping I might find some disreputable woman or some cast-off woman disreputable enough to take me in for the night. I knew I had no line of chatter, none. I just couldn't open up. I knew they thought I was unfriendly, that I had no rap. But it really wasn't that way at all. What did you say after you said Hi? You from around here? Why did they look so snotty when you tried to talk to them? Weren't they lonely, too? Didn't they want some warm flesh to press up against? I didn't know any of the answers. I'd met my wife on a blind double date. We'd gotten pretty well acquainted in the back seat before we ever got out of her daddy's driveway.

The young lady who was barmaiding smiled when she came over to pick up my empty.

"Another Bud, please."

She stuck the empty in a cardboard case and bent over the cooler for a fresh one.

"Here you go. Dollar fifty."

I paid and waved away the change. What was wrong with

me? No rap at all. My ex-wife was probably getting all the good loving she needed. I couldn't understand why the male had to court the female. Was what she had better to him than what he had was to her? I didn't think so. I thought it was an equal thing. And then of course there was the question of homosexuality and lesbianism. Whips and chains, foot fetishes, all that other kinky stuff you read about.

I saw a boy I sometimes painted houses with, and went over and stood by him. Like me he wasn't much of a talker.

"Hey."

"Hey."

"How's it going?"

"All right. You?"

"Pretty good. You need a beer?"

"Nah."

We watched some people shoot pool for a while. I didn't even know why I was up there. I always expected something to happen and it never did. It wasn't going to, not to me. I turned to leave and the guy I'd seen earlier was in my face. I've had it happen before.

"I don't like your face."

"Oh yeah? Tough shit."

He swung. I ducked. He swung again. I ducked again.

"Hey, man. You're drunk. Why don't you fuck off?"

He swung again. This time he hit one of the cedar posts with his fist. I heard his hand break. It took the starch out of him right away. I saw then that he wasn't some badass who could kick the shit out of anybody he wanted to. He was just a wimp with a broken hand.

He went down on his knees and did quite a bit of howling, holding his hand. I could have kicked him as hard as I wanted to, right on the side of his head, or on the back of his neck. I just stood there and watched him, and enjoyed it, which is one of the negative traits of my character, I suppose.

35

I was up there another night and some old guy was collapsed over the bar, mumbling and muttering to himself. I bought a beer and stood close to him. If you tuned out the television and the guys shooting pool and the stereo and the MTV you could hear what he was saying. He looked about seventy, ragged coat, untrimmed hair, disreputable shoes. Just about what I knew I'd look like in thirty more years if I kept going the way I was going. Have none of my work published and be an old wasted guy, bitter at the world. It wasn't a very pretty picture.

"Nineteen sixty-six," he said. He shook his head viciously and stared at his beer bottle with murder in his eyes. "You. Her. Everybody. The whole world. Yeah. The whole world knows. And what good did it do to try? Huh? Three goddamn weeks. Only time when you was little it did any good to try and talk to you. Just one right after another. Keep on hoping and hoping and it don't do no good. It ain't no way. Never will be. Grow their hair and smoke cigarettes and run off away from home and get in trouble and call wanting money. Or sell your ass in the street. Just make more like you. Don't even know how many. Gather em up and send em off to China or Africa or somewhere don't nobody know you."

I leaned against the bar next to him. "Emptiness," I said. "That hollow feeling. The empathy of the whole world or the uncaring glance of a businessman in a car. Trying to sell newspapers with gum stuck on your shoe. Raining. Cold hard snow ice sleet falling from the sky. A biscuit and no jelly to put in it."

I looked at him. He looked at me. He looked back at his beer.

"She had geraniums," he said. "Little black notebooks crammed full of em. You couldn't tell how many." He shook his head. "I started counting one day at eleven forty-five p.m. and got up to three hundred and seventy-two and the door-bell rang. I went to the door, I was thinking, three seventy-two, three seventy-two, three seventy-two. Guy with a deliv-ery van out there. Had fourteen chrysanthemums for Mrs. Rose Dale Bourdeaux. Small guy, black, little pencil mous-tache. Sneaky eyes, trying to see all in the house behind me."

"Drunk," I said. "That's where I've been. Night after night after night. When even the whole world don't want to wake up and look at you. And why? Because they don't like it. Not in their house, not in their car, not in their church. Throw you in the garbage. Pick you up the next morning. Wipe you off and set you down and say, Boy, walk straight, now. Walk the straight and narrow. Walk the straight and narrow arrow."

"Shoot em all," he said. "Just line em up against the wall and line their goddamn drivers up too and give em forty whacks. What they did to that guy out there in Utah. Made him feel better. It let all that poison out of him. He had that poison in him and it wasn't no way for it to get out except when he went to the bathroom and then just a little bit at a time. His body was making more poison than it could get rid of. It was making about two quarts a day and this was in the wintertime."

"They should have bottled it and sold it," I said.

"What?"

"His poison."

"Oh no. No no. No no no no no. There ain't a container made that'll hold it. It won't ride in a truck. First thing you know it'll have done fell off and rolled down the hill and busted open. Then where would you be? Little kids running around stepping in it. No, you best not bottle it," he said.

I shut up. He wasn't looking at me any more. He had said his last sentence with a finality that left no room for discussion. I didn't try to engage him in any more conversation, and after a while, after looking around the whole room fearfully for a while, he hurried out.

36

I started having wet dreams at night and sometimes in the daytime. I'd have these tremendous ejaculations that felt like lumps of lava flowing down my urethra. And it would always be on the verge of putting it in. I never got to put it in. The sight of her titties or something, maybe just her puss, would make me skeet off. Wake up with wet underwear and just moan and turn over. But I often had fantasies about women while I was awake. I would imagine a whole elaborate scene with dirty dialogue, just construct a short erotic film in my head.

I wasn't hearing anything from my work. I had plenty of money, but not much desire. I was drinking more and writing less. I read the reviews of books in the local papers and noted what was on the best-seller list each week. I dreamed dreams of having my stories published in magazines and having my name on the covers of books, things the people I was raised around had never thought of. I knew people who were illiterate or nearly so and drank with them. One day I rode across the river with a boy who lived near me to get some beer. He was a pulpwood hauler but he knew that I wrote, somehow. He wore a T-shirt thick with sawdust and the cooler in the floor of his truck was full of beer already, but it was Friday and he'd been paid for two loads that day and he just came by the house and asked me to ride over there with him. It turned out he wrote poetry and wanted me to read some of it. The more I talked to him, the more I found out about him. He wasn't from around here. He'd been educated at Washington University and he had a degree in neurobiology but had decided suddenly that he didn't want to do that. Now he was cutting pulpwood, risking his life and neck every day for pine logs, and writing poetry at night. His name was Thomas Slade, and he told me he was ready to start writing a novel.

Once we were in the road, he gave me a beer, and I smoked cigarettes and started reading his poems. They had a strange meter and rhyme and his words were good. We didn't talk while I read them. We drank beer and enjoyed the sunshine and the feeling that maybe two kindred souls were about to come together. The first poem was about his father, who was an alcoholic, and it had some vivid images. It was strong and

I told him so. The next one was about a family of children whose father ran over a squirrel in the road, and they all screamed until he stopped. The guts were squashed out of it but it was still alive. The father had to stop and back over it a couple of times to kill it. It was a really good poem and I told him so. He smiled shyly, but I could tell that he was pleased. We had a Stihl 041 Farm Boss chainsaw on the seat between us. Jugs of oil and gasoline were on the floorboard. I was really starting to enjoy myself.

We got pulled over two miles this side of the beer joint by a state trooper. We'd been listening to Patsy Cline on his tape player. It was just sort of hammered into the dash with wires hanging everywhere, but it played, and he had some excellent speakers hung from the roof of the cab with coat hangers. We'd been moving and grooving and wailing with Patsy, God bless her soul, slammed into the side of a mountain so many years ago. My driver had had several beers, which the trooper smelled after he noticed that Thomas had no lights of any kind on his truck. He didn't have an inspection sticker either. His tires were like soft shit. I knew we wouldn't get off lightly.

I stayed in the truck while he talked to the man. While he walked the line. While he closed his eyes and leaned his head back and walked a line backwards down the side of the road. While he did ten push-ups and clapped his hands together under his chest each time he came up. After all that the man let us go. Told us to "get them fuckin lights fixed." Seemed disgruntled that he couldn't carry us to jail. Well, he had his job, and we had ours.

We made it on over to the beer joint in good time, considering we'd been messed with by the Troopers of Control, the most motivated, energetic, dead-set-on-catching-folks-like-me highway boys ever farted in a cruiser. There were lots of other folks over there. I latched or tried to latch onto what appeared to be a woman but turned out to be a fourteen-year-old girl and got told right quick by her brother, who was large, that she was underage. He was like seventeen himself. It made me feel old.

I wandered around for a while. I started having a sinking spell. It helped to hold onto posts and stuff. And a whole lot of stuff happened that I don't remember. People kept handing me beers. I guess old Thomas Slade was paying for them, but I don't remember. I never did find out, though, since that was the last time I talked to him. While passed out on the seat, late that night, going home, I woke up, saw some lights, heard something hit, and then we flipped over about eight times. I kept rolling around from the seat to the floor. Things were flying and hitting me in the head. I guess some of them were old Thomas Slade's Patsy Cline tapes. He had about nine of them.

I woke up again as some firemen were pulling the truck apart with the Jaws of Life. There was a long wrapped white bundle on the ground that was Thomas Slade. I, miraculously, was not injured much. Five-inch cut on my wrist, three-inch cut on my forehead. Thomas had his spine broken and his head crushed, and I saw that he wouldn't be cutting any more pine trees, or writing any more beautiful poetry.

37

I was getting pretty sick of death. It canceled a lot of checks. It snuck up on people who thought they didn't have time for it, laid families to waste who had just bought a new house. It caused problems miles down the road for children and everybody else. I didn't know what I was worrying about it for. It was going to get me one day, and there wasn't anything I could do about it. Death was going to put the bite on everybody, even if it did sometimes bite before its time. It got Raymond, and I knew he wasn't ready to go. It made me sick for it to get Gardner, just cruising on his Harley before his marriage. It made me sick, death did. I'd buried lots of my own. I was afraid I might have to bury Alisha. I was afraid they might have to bury me. I didn't want Alan to see that. I wanted him to go out to Uncle Lou's and stay a few weeks, learn to rope and ride, trim the horses' feet, how to brush their hair so it's most pleasing to them. I had a whole lot of faith, but I hadn't been to church in a while. God probably didn't recognize me because He hadn't seen me in so long in His house. I felt sort of slime ball, sort of scuz bag, sort of piss-complected puke. I felt like I'd make almost anybody barf. So I skipped town for a few days.

38

It wasn't any better down the road. This place I checked into charged thirty dollars a week rent. But I thought I might really get into the underside of life there and find something to write about. I was sort of undercover. There was a small wading pool out back where guests could sit around in their lawn chairs and drink beer. I did this several evenings. Most of the people there were old, like they didn't have anywhere else to go, or maybe it was just a decrepit nursing home. I didn't know what I was doing there with them. I had a home of my own, so why was I sitting around drinking beer with a bunch of old people? Looking at leaves in a wading pool? I knew I needed to go home and check my mail. But I could hardly bear to go back to my loud empty rooms.

After I'd been there two days I saw a fight. Two old guys who couldn't do much, just pushing and shoving at first. But they were cussing plenty. If they could have fought as well as they could cuss they'd have both wound up in the hospital or the morgue. They were filling the air with oaths that reeked of filth and vulgarity. It nearly embarrassed me myself.

One of the old guys shoved the other old guy down and that ended the physical part of the fight. I looked at the loser. He was sitting on the ground, trying to get up. The victor was walking away. He was swaggering a little. You could tell he thought he was hot shit on toast. I didn't know what they'd been fighting over. I didn't want to know. I just wanted the old guy who'd been pushed down to stop cussing so much. He was slinging one motherfucker after another one to the point where it went past ugly. I knew God was up there hearing it. I put my sunglasses on.

After a while the old guy on the ground got up and went inside. I kept sitting there drinking my beer, looking at the leaves in the pool. It needed cleaning really badly, but nobody seemed to want to do it. I damn sure didn't want to do it.

I vacated the place a few hours later, wondering when things would come to some kind of end. I was restless and couldn't stay still. I wasn't happy at home and I wasn't happy away from home. It looked like there was nothing to do but *go* home. So that's where I went, a little reluctantly.

39

I stayed drunk for a few days and didn't really notice a lot of what was happening around me. The phone rang a few times, usually while I was in bed. People would try to talk to me and I would try to talk to them, but we couldn't understand each other, so I'd hang up. I lost track of the days. I didn't know if a particular day was Sunday or Saturday, or Tuesday. I went to the refrigerator once to see if there was anything there to eat, but there was nothing there, so I crawled back to bed. I left beer in the freezer compartment and it froze and burst and ran down the front of the refrigerator. I put more beer in, overslept, and it froze and burst. I knew I'd have to sober up sometime and clean it up, but I wasn't ready to yet. I wanted to get that drunk over with and let things go back to normal if they could.

I tried to write a poem about Thomas Slade while I was drunk. The poem was no good. I tried to write two other poems, about Jerome and Kerwood White, while I was drunk, but they were no good either. I rode around drunk, walked around drunk, slept and woke up drunk. I wrote drunk, ate

drunk, washed my hair drunk. I watched television drunk as
a boiled owl. I went over to Monroe's house drunk one day to
see him while he was at work and his mother didn't appreciate it worth a damn. I knew better. It was just that drunk had
done me in. I considered going to see my mother drunk but I
knew that wouldn't do, either. I thought about going to see
Marilyn drunk, but I knew that would just reinforce her belief
that I was nothing but a drunk. And I thought about going to
see my uncle drunk, but I wasn't too drunk to know that he'd
probably haul off and knock the hell out of me, things being
what they were and sacrifices being as valuable as they were,
and all the shit I'd blown to him about blah blah blah. I wound
up just going back home drunk, drinking some more, and
going to bed.

I had a nightmare that night. I was drunk in the nightmare, with a whole lot of other people who were drunk in a
large log pen. There were hogs walking around. They had
caught all of us out on the highways drunk. The hogs had
been in the trailer of a drunk truck driver. All of us had been
sentenced to death. Society was going to be rid of this problem with no qualms. We were being killed one at a time, and
the whole world was watching. Some were shot, some were
hanged, some were stabbed with long sharp knives. Two guys
in front of me got it with axes. There were bodies left and
right. Whoever was in charge of the thing was selling beer in
there, too, just to see what would happen, I guess. Everybody was sober by then, and the beer stand wasn't getting
much business.

They had a huge slave chained to a tree stump in the line I

was in. The people went forward one at a time, after hand-cuffs were put on them. The slave rested on his axe handle until their necks were across the stump. Then he swung it and grunted and the bloody head of the axe flashed through the air and there was a loud *THWACK!*

They led me to the stump. My toes were squishing in blood. They handcuffed me and forced me down on the bloody wood. Splinters dug into my throat. I tried to move but they held me down. I turned my head sideways toward the slave. His feet moved, and he grunted, and bloody mud splashed from between his toes.

40

I woke at daybreak. Nighthawks were calling softly in the stillness, and it was cool. I got up. There was one can of frozen orange juice in the freezer compartment, frozen beer all over it. I ran the water in the sink until it got hot and then I thawed the orange juice out partway, holding it under the running water. I found a pitcher, opened the can, and put the yellow lump into it. I took a steak knife and tried to chop it up into smaller pieces. I measured out three cans of hot water and poured them in and stirred it, my tongue so dry I couldn't lick my lips, or bear to. There were some ice cubes in the trays. I filled a glass with cubes and poured the orange juice over it and got my cigarettes and lighter and went out to the front porch in my underwear and sat in a chair.

Fog was lifting off the river. Crows were rising from the

fog. Cars with their headlights on were going down the highway. The trees were mantled with mist, standing dark with
their heavy rafts of leaves. I drank some of the orange juice,
and it was like a parched man two days in the desert being
offered a drink from a well. It was that good. I lit a cigarette, and the smoke hurt my lungs. The things I did to myself
were stupid, and without reason, or for reasons that I only
imagined, slights I imagined had been done by the world,
never my own fault. I knew the kids were sleeping somewhere, their eyes closed, their breathing shallow. In sleep
their long lashes were easy to see, faces I'd kissed again and
again.

I put my face in my hand, and I cried, and promised myself
that I would try to do better, for me, for everybody, for the
kids especially. I hoped the promise would last.

41

The money started running low again, due to drinking and
smoking too much and being a generous guy with drinks for
drunks who had no money. There were people I knew who
could make their way to a bar with no money, but sit there
and drink by careful and calculated cunning. I couldn't do it,
but I knew plenty of people who did. I decided to write interesting stories about them, stay home, drink less. But when I
got to writing all those drinking stories, it made me want to
get drunk myself while I was writing them. So what I wound
up doing was writing them in the *bar*, with my pencils and
notebook and papers all spread out everywhere. And I'd sit

there and smoke and have cigarette ashes thumped all over everything, be smoking like a fiend, scribbling all these words. They knew I was trying to put out some good stuff and nobody messed with me. They were proud of having me write in their bar. They didn't know any published authors. But they knew one unpublished author.

There was a little chickadee who started working in there. My heart sank the first time I saw her, because I knew I could never have her. She was just too good for me. She had long brown hair and she had on a jogging suit bottom with a red striped T-shirt over the top. She had a shy way of smiling when she talked to the other guys around the bar. Her beauty broke my heart.

I was deep into some things about two guys fresh out of the penitentiary and some other guys moose-hunting with secret dopers in the Great Pacific Northwest and another little thing about dead children who got up and walked at night, when she came over and asked me what I was writing. This was after she had seen me do this for a couple of nights in a row.

"I, uh, I'm writing some stories," I said, and shielded my work with my hand. "Could I get another beer?"

She smiled her shy little smile and got the beer for me, smiling while she was reaching in the cooler, smiling when she put it up on the bar in front of me. I laid two dollars on the bar. She took one and pushed the other one back.

"Happy Hour," she said, and I looked and it was four o'clock.

"Thanks," I said. I folded the other dollar and put it in her jar.

For the next thirty minutes I wrote. I heard a couple of carpenter types come in a few times and wonder aloud what that motherfucker was doing over there in the corner, but I didn't pay any attention to that because it was to be expected. I'd paid for my space and I figured I could use it like I wanted to, as long as I wasn't dealing dope or selling insurance. I was trying to decide whether or not to let a story have an ambiguous ending, and also fretting over tone and symbolism in one particular piece, when she came back over.

"You're Leon Barlow, aren't you?" she said.

I just barely looked up. I knew I couldn't get over with her. "Yeah, I'm him," I said, and looked back down at my papers.

"You know Monroe, don't you?"

"Yeah."

"He's the one told me you wrote. He was talking to me the other night about you. He said you were a real good writer."

I didn't say, Well, the world's out to fuck me. I said: "Well, I haven't had anything published."

"I'd sure like to read some of your stuff sometime. I love to read."

I looked at her. That sweet little mouth. Fine little ass. Smooth skin I knew like my hand had never felt. Marilyn's was lumpy and had scabs on it, stretch marks and cellulite and pones on her feet, plus she stunk up the bathroom something terrible. I figured this dainty thing didn't even have to shit but just farted little fragrant poots when she had to. I didn't know what a real dick would do to her. Probably kill her. I looked back down at my work.

"I don't let nobody look at my stuff except Monroe," I muttered.

42

Alisha died right after that. They said it was crib death, SIDS, but I don't think that's what it was. I thought it was punishment to me for giving up my wife and my family and all the wrath of God howling after me all the days of my life to the ends of the earth. I wanted to go out into the forest and live like a madman with leaves for clothes and live in a hole in the ground and throw rocks at anybody who came near.

My whole family was there. I was stunned with all the marijuana and liquor I could stuff into myself and still remain standing. I signed papers, made promises, heard prayers and screaming and gnashing of teeth. Cried till my eyes were sore. I took on a pain that would never leave me, never let me rest until years had passed, and then it would always remain like lead that had settled in the bottom of my heart, a little sad face smiling up, reminding me always, even when I lay on my deathbed, Alisha, born wrong, Alisha, child of God, Alisha a soul wafting out across space with her tiny hands clapping.

43

I got drunk and thrown in jail. They let me out, I got drunk again, they threw me in again. I had ample time to reflect upon my situation. It hadn't been DUI, just public drunk, and then it wouldn't have happened if I hadn't happened to smart off to the arresting officers. They got me going down the street the first time and then coming *up* the street the second time. Same street.

There were quite a few jailbirds in there, people doing long time. Everybody had the option of doing community service and reducing their sentences by half, but hardly anybody wanted to. I guess they were sorry, plus they had two squares a day and television, game shows mostly. I put up with it for two days, and then I told them to let me go pick up some trash or something.

They put me to helping an old lady cook food for the prisoners in a kitchen halfway across town. She seemed suspicious of me at first, but I kept my nails clean and washed my hands a lot and said ma'am to her, and before long she was smiling and laughing and telling me about her grown kids. We talked a lot. I told her about Alisha. She let me eat all the time, and there was good stuff in there she fixed for me that the prisoners in the jail never saw. Ham, steaks, catfish. I washed pots and pans and wore a white apron and sat on the back steps sometimes, smoking cigarettes while the free people walked down the sidewalk next to the bank.

There was a bar just down the alley that happened to be mine, and I'd sit out there watching the people going in and

out, free as birds. I could see the exact spot where they'd
nabbed me. There was a large Dempsey Dumpster that the
cops hid behind and leaped out and grabbed drunks from,
guys just trying to make their way back to their cars and sleep
it off. It was the same method they'd used on me. She saw
me sitting out there one afternoon and asked me what I was
looking at.

"I'm just watching those people," I said.

I could feel her standing behind me. Her husband had
died of a heart attack the year before, the year before he'd
been going to retire. They'd been planning on opening a small
cafe together in their retirement years. They'd had it planned
for over ten years. Now she was cooking two meals a day for
the county.

"Why don't you go down there and drink you a beer?" she
said. "Might help you get rid of the blues. If they come check
on you I'll tell them I sent you to the store for me."

"I ain't got any money. They took it all away from me in the
jail."

A five-dollar bill slid down over my left shoulder and
stopped right in front of my pocket. I twisted my head around
and looked at her. She was smiling down on me like an extra
grandmother. I put my fingers on the money and held her
hand for a moment.

"My baby died, too," she said. "Forty years ago. I can handle it for a couple of hours."

I wanted to cry because I felt so damn good that there was
such kindness in the world. Instead I got up and took off my
apron. I hung it on the nail where I always hung it and looked

at her. She was stirring stuff on the stove, and the steam was rising off her pots and pans.

I went to her and hugged her shoulders. She shook her head, patted me on the hand. I went out the door and down the alley, looking both ways for cars, looking all ways for cops from the jail. I'd found out that once they got after you, they tended to stay after you, and I didn't want them after me any more.

The Happy Hour light was on. Beer was a dollar. If I drank fast I could get five down in a couple of hours. On the other hand, if I was obviously drunk when I went back to the jail, I'd probably get the nice old lady in trouble, might even cause her to lose her meal contract with the county. It was a dilemma, and I hated dilemmas. I sat down on a bar stool and waited for somebody to wait on me.

There weren't many people in there. A couple of guys in business suits, a couple more in carpenter's overalls. Two middle-aged women with sunglasses who pulled them down and looked over the tops of them at me when I sat down. I wondered if it would be possible for me to make a break for it while I was out on my own like that. I only had three more days to serve, which actually meant a day and a half if I stayed in the kitchen with the sweet old lady. I was tired of listening to all the shit in the jail every night, though, lying there on that one-inch mattress and looking up at the ceiling. There were also some homosexual things going on in there at night that I didn't particularly like to hear.

Sweet thing popped up from behind the counter. She grinned real big when she saw me.

"Well, hey," she said. She came over and laced her fingers together on the bar. "Where you been so long?"

"Jail. Can I get a Bud?"

She got the bottle for me and gave me four back from my five.

"Monroe told me you were in jail but I didn't believe him. I thought he was just playing with me. What'd you do?"

"Walked down the street. Had a little too much to drink. Got smart with a fucking officer of the law."

I was looking everywhere but at her, and she was steady watching me. I didn't know why. I knew I looked awful. I hadn't had a shave in about nine days and I knew my teeth were beyond funky. I knew I had to get my shit together pretty soon because this wasn't getting it, no sir.

"So how much longer you got to go?"

"Couple of days. Three, I think. Can I get another beer?"

I shouldn't have been drinking that fast, but I was. At that rate I could make Happy Hour live up to its name. She got the beer and pushed away the dollar. I said to myself, Hmmmm.

She went back behind the counter and started doing some other stuff. I had some generic cigarettes and I lit one of them. It tasted like a selected blend of dried horse turds. I didn't want to go back to jail. I didn't see how I could. I thought again about making a break. It would have been easy. All I had to do was walk out of town and stick out my thumb. But I knew they'd finally get me back, and it would probably be worse when they did. I sat there drinking. I drank two more. The little sweet thing kept smiling at me, but I've always somehow had this look on my face that makes people stay away. I don't mean for it to be there. I don't even know it's there. But people have told me they've seen it before, and that it doesn't look friendly. If I knew how to get rid of it I would.

Finally I went on back to my kitchen. I had one dollar left. I gave it to her. She just smiled and patted my hand.

44

I laid on my rack at the jail that night and looked at the ceiling some more. People had written things all over it with either cigarette lighters or matches. Ugly things, sexual things, the ugliest things you could imagine and some you couldn't. They never turned the lights off in there, let them stay on twenty-four hours a day. It made it very hard to sleep.

I didn't feel like a criminal, but here I was in with criminals. Some had stolen, some had killed or nearly killed people, some like me had just been caught publicly drunk. I would have written something if I'd had anything to write on, but finally I just went to sleep.

45

They let me out a couple of days later. I felt about as shabby as I'd felt in a while, unshaven, dirty, shamed. Nobody told me not to come back any more. I knew they were memorizing my face so they could nab me again the next time I even thought about fucking up.

I walked outside. It was hot. I'd neglected to ask them if they'd towed my car, so I decided to walk back to the parking lot and see if it was still there.

It was a long way over there on foot. I almost got run over a few times. Everybody seemed to be going somewhere in a hurry. It was dangerous to step off the curb that day.

My old car was sitting all by itself in the middle of the parking lot. The tires were low. Somebody'd ripped off the radio antenna. It looked sort of sad and forlorn. I was just hoping it would crank.

I opened the door and got in and sat down. The seats were burning hot. I put the key in and turned it over, and it went waw, awaw, waw. I let it rest a minute. Both of us had been through a lot. I was afraid I'd have to be jumped off, but I didn't have any cables, and there didn't seem to be anybody familiar around with a fresh hot battery. I said Lord, please.

I turned it over again and it coughed and farted and finally ran. I sat there revving it up. The bar across the street was closed. I wondered if the little sweet thing would be there that night. I wondered if I went home and cleaned up and showered and shaved and cut my fingernails and brushed my teeth, if it would be possible for me to get over with her. Then I looked at myself and said Naaaaaaa.

I looked at the gas gauge. It was damn near on empty, and I only had two dollars on me. However, I still had some of Uncle Lou's money stashed.

I limped out of town, almost whipped, my head hanging,

and my hopes not too high. I wasn't completely beaten. I just needed a breather in between rounds.

46

My house hadn't burned down or anything while I'd been gone. There were a few notes from Monroe tacked on the front door. One of them said WHERE YOU AT? I'VE BEEN BY HERE THREE TIMES ALREADY. LET'S GO DRINK A BEER ONE NIGHT, MONROE. Another one said, I HEARD YOU WERE IN JAIL. I AIN'T GOT ANY MONEY OR I'D COME GET YOU OUT, MONROE. The last one said, LYNN SAID SHE SAW YOU THE OTHER DAY AND SHE SAID YOU SAID YOU WERE IN JAIL. IF YOU DON'T GET OUT PRETTY SOON I'LL SEE IF I CAN BORROW SOME MONEY FROM MAMA AND COME GET YOU OUT, MONROE. P.S. IF YOU WERE IN JAIL HOW COME THEY LET YOU GO DRINK BEER?

I threw the notes in the trash and looked in the refrigerator. There just happened to be a couple of cold ones in there. I wondered who Lynn was and then realized she must have been the sweet little thing I wanted to murder with my dick. I got one of the beers and sat down on the couch and pulled my boots off. Just as soon as I did that, I realized that I had about nine days' worth of mail stacked up in my mailbox. I left my beer on the coffee table and went down the driveway, my feet tender on the gravel, saying Ouch, damn, shit. The mailbox was crammed full of shit, a lot of it manila envelopes of my own fiction that had found its way home. There were letters from my ex-wife's lawyer, letters from the funeral home, letters from the tombstone people. There was even a letter from the jail that had beat me home. I scooped it all out, didn't examine it too closely, and carried it all back to the house, hot-footing it over the gravel, saying Oh, fuck, oo. My feet were too tender. I never did spend enough time going barefooted. Marilyn used to, though. Her feet were tough as hell. She could walk over nails, gravel, anything. She could lay a fucking on you, too. She really knew how to do it. She really knew how to get pregnant, too. She was about six and a half months gone when we finally got married. Her daddy wanted to shoot somebody, I think. On the other hand, I guess he was just glad to have somebody finally claim her.

I got back to the house and collapsed on the couch with my mail, sucked down a big drink of the beer, and tossed out everything that didn't pertain to my writing. The first thing I noticed was a manila envelope that I had sent off with a story inside that had come back without the story inside, which I knew meant something. I didn't know if it meant what I was hoping it meant. It might not have meant anything at all. But it just happened to be from *Ivory Towers*, home of the great or maybe not-so-great Betti DeLoreo. I was in a quandary as to opening it. I was scared to open it and scared not to open it. I had self-addressed the thing, true, and the great et cetera had sent it back to me minus my story. I could tell the story wasn't inside it. I held it up to the light, but I couldn't see a thing through the manila. What did it mean? Had she taken my story? Was everything fixing to be worth it? Had I broken through? Or had they just lost my story and were writing to apologize for it? It was hard to stand the pressure. I ripped the envelope open. There, inside, in Betti DeLoreo's own handwriting, was a note to me:

Dear Leon,

I like your story a lot up here but I'm having trouble convincing the senior editor that we ought to publish it. I know this is very unorthodox to do this, but I want to keep it around here a while and nag him every chance I get. The only thing is, if I nag him too much, he'll get pissed off and reject the story. I have to work on him real slowly and bring it up gradually. He's trying to write his master's thesis right now and things are very bad for him. However, your story, "Raping the Dead," is a big favorite around here and a lot of people who don't have the power to accept or reject a story like it. If I owned this magazine we'd publish it. Please have some patience. Your work is difficult and complex and everybody doesn't understand it. I think it scared some people and some people are jealous of it too and some are failed writers or struggling writers and it's just very hard to explain. I don't like seeing the infighting that goes on here, and I hate to see good work by an unknown author rejected in favor of bad work by an established one. I want to give you all the encouragement I can. You're too good a writer to remain unknown forever. You have to hang in there and if this tale does get rejected then you just have to send it out to

somebody else. Write me, please. Or send something
else. If this one doesn't make it, maybe another one will.
Please don't give up.

> All *very* warmest wishes,
> Betti DeLoreo

Well, well well well well well. Shit.

74

The sun went down late that evening like it always does. I
was sitting out on the front porch marveling at the way it lit
up the sky. It was pretty beautiful, and I didn't know what I'd
done to deserve it. Just sitting at the right time in the right
place, I guess.

I saw Monroe coming down the highway, and I saw him
turn into the driveway. I knew he probably had a trunk full of
cold beer. That was all right with me. He pulled up and
stopped beside the house and hung his head out the window,
and he was drunk as a by God.

"Mone get in," he said. "Ride you aroun a while."

"You got anything to drink? You look like you done drank it
all up."

He nodded his head and almost went to sleep hanging out
the window. I knew better than to get in with him.

"Get ya drank, bro. Mone. Ride you roun a while. Get you
drank a while."

He was waving a beer can around the whole time he was
saying that, sloshing beer out.

I got in with him. We just sat there in the car for five minutes. Finally he spoke.

"Wanna tell you summin. Made me mad, them mufuggers
put my bro in jail. Ain't right. Din have nobody ride aroun
with. Rode aroun by myself. Talk myself."

"You feeling all right, man?" I said.

"What? Kme? Lin. Em mufuggers put you in jail, again,
you caw me. I'll come up and get in jail too. Keep you compny.
Play cards. Yona beer?"

"I got one," I said.

"Good." He pulled the shift lever down into reverse. "We
gone ride aroun some."

"Can you drive, man?"

"Drive fine. Lin. Mufuggers give you shit, you caw me. I
got a ungle, Ungle Dick! Ungle Dick has been messin with
them sumbitches years. Stick at money in back pocket, see.
Rest you, ain't shit."

He'd backed over a couple of discarded bicycles by then,
but I didn't say anything. I reached over and put my foot on
the brake, stopped the car, and pulled it down into drive.

"Thain you. We gone ride aroun while. Got date later.
Cain't stay long, gotta picker up at six. Ain't stay long. What
time it?"

It looked at my watch. It was six-thirty and the gloam hadn't
even started yet. I had about half of a hot beer.

"You got any cold beer?"

We'd started rolling down the driveway, but he slammed
on the brakes and we slid in the gravel. He ratcheted the
shift lever back and forth for a while until he got it into

reverse. He started backing up the driveway. I reached over and stepped on the brake.

"You got any beer?"

"What?"

"You got any cold beer?"

He opened the door and fell out. I stepped on the brake a little harder and put it up in park. He was crawling in the gravel, heading for the trunk, muttering something.

I got out and asked him why didn't he just let me drive, but he didn't answer me. I had to help him back into the car. It wasn't even dark yet. I got him onto the back seat and stretched him out. About the cold beer I'd been right. The trunk was full of it.

I got one and got into the driver's seat.

"Who's your date with, man?"

"Wha?"

"Who's your date with?"

"Vemma. You know Vemma?"

"Velma? Velma White?"

"Yeah. Less go pick up Vemma."

He had his eyes closed talking to me. I didn't know why he'd chosen to get so fucked up right before a date. I was hoping he wasn't supposed to meet her parents.

"Tell you what, man. Why don't you give me her number? I'll call her and tell her you can't make it."

"Naw. Naw. Naw. Just dry me on over to Vemma's house. Vemma's gossum good pussy. Vemma's in love a me. Vemma thinks you a goodlookin summitch. We'll double date. Go on over Vemma's."

I started driving. I didn't figure it mattered where I drove to. I was sober anyway. I had a joint that I'd rolled up earlier, and I pulled it out of my pocket and lit it. I had all that cold beer to drink, and I figured I could handle it for a few hours. That would be about enough time for him to sleep it off. I didn't want to interfere with his love life, but I remembered where Velma lived. I decided to go in a roundabout way over there.

Monroe had some good tapes, and as quick as the buzz hit me, I started playing them. I felt good about taking care of him in the back seat.

Night closed in. It came slowly, and we rode down by the river and I looked at the hawks perched on the high limbs in the trees and saw a huge owl come out of the woods and find a single light wire with his talons and sit there swiveling his head after me as we drove by. Life seemed pretty fine. I didn't have a woman like he did, but I could at least enjoy riding around. Marilyn had always questioned it. We never had been able to get along. It always seemed that she thought what I was doing was nothing, that it would never amount to anything, and so far it hadn't. I hadn't sold anything, hadn't published one word. Maybe I never would, but Betti DeLoreo didn't seem to think so. I got to thinking about her again. I knew I didn't need to, because I knew that if I really knew what she really looked like, I'd probably be disappointed. She'd probably have tartar on her teeth or something. I decided we'd better ride by Velma's house at least and see if the light was on. I'd entertained the idea of stopping and explaining things to her, let her see him in the back seat so she'd know I wasn't lying.

We rode by there four times. The light was on each time. I knew she was probably pissed.

"Hey, man," I said. "You awake?"

Silence from the back seat.

"Hey, man! You awake?"

He wasn't doing anything but sleeping, and I knew it wouldn't go over well with her. I decided to stop anyway. I whipped it around in the middle of the road and went back to her house. I pulled up in front like I belonged there—after all, I did—and sat down on the horn. Nothing happened for about two minutes. Then somebody came to the front door and peeked out. Then another person came and peeked out. I figured the second one was probably her daddy with a gun. I let off the horn.

I already had it in reverse when she came out the door. She had on white pants and a black blouse, and she had a purse with her. I hated I'd even stopped.

"Hey, Velma," I said. "I'm Leon. Remember me?"

She poked her head in the car. I turned on the interior light so she could see him.

"What's the matter with him?" she said. She looked at her watch. "He's two hours late."

"I believe he's having a little sinking spell. I'm surprised you waited this long."

"What'd you do? Take him off and get him drunk?"

I thought about it. I remembered how nasty she'd been when her brothers got killed, but that had been understandable. On the other hand, I didn't know why Monroe was messing around with her, even though he'd said that her nooky was excellent. That was probably true, based on the fact that the worst I've ever had was wonderful.

"Yeah," I said. "I tied him down and taped a funnel on his mouth and then poured ten Old Milwaukees down him. Then I poured four shots of peppermint schnapps down him. Then I poured two shots of whiskey down him. Then I poured a snifter of brandy down him. Then I poured two martinis down him. Then he puked. But I kept pouring it down him. Then I opened a bottle of tequila."

"Oh bullshit," she said. She went around to the passenger side and got in. "Just drive me uptown," she said. "I'll get him sobered up after awhile. You got a beer in here?"

"Trunk's full of it."

"Well, how about getting me one out?"

"That your daddy looking out the window?"

"Yeah. He watches me like a hawk now. Where's that beer?"

The ice broke after she got one down her. I had a little of the joint left and we shared that. By the time we got to town we were laughing and talking and singing along with Monroe's tapes. I felt a little guilty, but he was still sleeping on the back seat. When we got to the bar he was still asleep, and she had wormed her way over next to me in the seat. When we pulled up and stopped, she said she didn't really want to go in, and could we ride around a little longer? I said sure.

I can't remember anything that happened after that. I know a lot of things happened, but I can't remember what they were.

48

We were in a ditch when we woke up. It was muddy, and we had mud all over us. Mud was all over the seats. It had caked on the dash, on our clothes, on the headliner. We were way up in the woods somewhere, as usual. The sun was shining. It was nine o'clock in the morning. My mouth felt like a wad of cotton, and mosquitoes had feasted on us all night long. He was still asleep on the back seat. I woke him up and we flipped a coin to see who'd walk out to the road and flag somebody down to come pull us out. He won. Or lost.

49

I slept for about two days and then I went back to work on my work. I thought about painting a few houses just to keep my hand in and help tide me over when winter came but I could hardly bring myself to do it. It was hard to turn loose some of that freedom. That old freedom was nice.

Raoul came by to see me one day but I wouldn't let him in. He could see me, and I could see him, but I just kept sitting at my typewriter, pecking words out, and he started knocking and it went on for a long time. He shouted something, several things, but I didn't listen. I'd about decided not to listen to anybody for the rest of my life. He kept knocking, and I got up and went over to the stereo and put Johnny Winter on and ignored him. He kept knocking. I started writing a story about a woman and a man with a little child going down a sidewalk late at night, the little girl in a long white dress and having to run to keep up with her mother and father, who were running from something beyond bad. I saw that it was on a dark street somewhere in New Jersey with the rain falling and I wondered what was going through the little girl's head. She was running to keep up, her mother barely holding her hand, her bare feet flying over the wet sidewalks, up and down over the curbs as they crossed the alleys. Her hair was long, brown, and her arm was stretched out in front of her as she held onto her mother's hand, and her feet were flying. I kept that image with me, desperation, flight, fear, until the knocking stopped and Raoul went away, I knew sadly. I went to the refrigerator and got a beer. I sat back down at my machine. I had to find out what they were running from. I had to find out if the little girl was going to be safe. I didn't know if she would be or not. But whatever it was she was running from, I knew I had to save her from it, and that I was the only one who could do it. They were running, running, the cars going by, and I could see the slippery sidewalks, and the lights in the stores, and I could see my mother and my father looking back over their shoulders at whatever was chasing us, and I ran as fast as I could, terrified, not knowing how it would end, knowing I had to know.